MW00933952

HER DRAGON DESTINY

BLACK CLAW DRAGONS: BOOK 5

Roxie Ray
© 2020

Disclaimer

This is a work of fiction. Names, places, characters and events are all fictitious for the reader's pleasure. Any similarities to real people, places, events, living or dead are all coincidental.

Contents

Chapter 1 - Bethany 5

Chapter 2 - Maddox 23

Chapter 3 - Bethany 37

Chapter 4 - Maddox 52

Chapter 5 - Bethany 68

Chapter 6 - Maddox 84

Chapter 7 - Bethany 104

Chapter 8 - Maddox 127

Chapter 9 - Bethany 146

Chapter 10 - Maddox 163

Chapter 11 - Bethany 184

Chapter 12 - Maddox 206

Chapter 13 - Bethany 222

Chapter 14 - Maddox 248

Chapter 15 - Bethany 266

Chapter 16 - Maddox 285

Chapter 17 - Bethany 297

Chapter 18 - Maddox 316

Chapter 19 - Bethany 337

Chapter 20 - Maddox 348

Chapter 21 - Bethany 359

Chapter 22 - Maddox 371

Chapter 23 - Bethany 380

Chapter 24 - Maddox 389

Chapter 25 - Rico...400

Chapter 1 - Bethany

Not for the first time, or even the second or third, I wished Kyle was here to help me make this decision. These houses were little goldmines, but it wasn't easy to know which ones were worth the time and energy.

Kyle always knew. From the first house we flipped, left to me by my grandparents, he'd had a knack for knowing which ones had strong bones and which ones would be more trouble than they were worth.

This one had been abandoned long ago. The longer a house went empty, the harder it was to bring back to life. Kyle had taught me that. He'd taught me so many things.

When my grandparents died and left me their swath of land—and the aging rental properties on them—my best friend Kyle had helped me figure out how to turn it into a thriving business. He'd been by my side, my closest confidante and advisor, since we were both kids.

But he was gone, and I still had a business to run. The rental properties were great income, but I didn't want to stop flipping. I'd been very lucky to find a contractor that I trusted to give me a fair, honest rate, as well as her opinions, without inflating numbers or padding her pockets.

But this morning, Kara had to go to one of the rentals to fix a leaking dishwasher and hadn't been able to come to look at the property. Instead, I took lots of pictures and notes, trying to remember everything Kyle had taught me, as well as filling out a checklist Kara had made for me and measuring everything. Then I measured it twice. Cut once, measure twice. Another lesson from Kyle.

If Kara liked my notes, we'd schedule a time with the property owner to get even more in-depth with the inspection.

I loved this part of the job. It was dusty and dirty and usually stinky. There were bugs and mud and mold. And yet, finding a house that was all of the above, yet could be brought back and rented to someone who needed a nice place to live at a fair price, or sold to someone who wanted an updated home without going through renovations themselves... That was truly the best part of the job.

Hopefully, Kara would be at the office when I returned so we could go over this data together. I had to make an offer on the house in a hurry. I wasn't the only flipper in the area, and it was a pretty stiff competition. The house had only been on the market for a day, so I hoped to seal the deal before the other guys even saw it.

It was hard enough to be the only female flipper in the area. Nobody trusted me to do the job right. Nobody'd ever questioned Kyle about his expertise, of course. Part of the knocks of being a woman in a world that was largely dominated by men.

But I'd maximized the potential of the property my grandparents left me. It was time to branch out.

After slipping the key back into the hiding spot, I hurried to my car once I was sure I had all the info I needed. The owner had trusted me to inspect the property on my own, which was nice. That was one of the few perks about being a woman. They didn't trust me to do a good job, but they didn't suspect me of duplicity, either.

Not that I would've ever cheated anyone. I'd been trying to build a reputation of being fair and honest. So far, so good. All it took was being fair and honest. Funny how that worked.

The property was just a few minutes from my home and office, so I beat Kara there. But I hadn't even had time to get my computer fired up when she walked in the door. My office was my favorite part of the house. It was full of plants and had a small fountain. I had my desk there, seats for anyone that I might need to have a meeting with, and a small area in the corner for my daughter to play in so she didn't get all up in Mommy's biz.

Kara sauntered in with a big smile on her face. "I got something for you."

Her body language was way too excited, so I sat up tall in my chair. "I love presents," I said. "What'd you get me?"

She pulled out a wooden sign with "Mom--Boss--CEO" hand-lettered on it.

I squealed and jumped up. "I love it!"

Kara had a hammer and nail in her hand, brought from her truck and ready to hang my new sign. I looked around and pointed to the spot I wanted it and beamed as she hung it. "That's amazing," I said. "Thank you."

She winked and plopped down in the plush chair across from my desk. "How was your date?"

My jaw dropped. I'd forgotten all about it. It had been such a weird experience that I'd brushed it off and hadn't given it another thought. Even when my mind drifted to it, I'd pushed it away and ignored it, purposefully not thinking about the date.

"I don't even know how to describe it. It was the most bizarre thing ever," I explained. "Harry, my date, and I had a nice time at the restaurant. So nice, we decided to go for ice cream."

Kara nodded eagerly. "Did he eat it off of your belly?"

What was it with my friends? My other friend, Abby, had said something of the same ilk. "No," I exclaimed. "Though, I did consider it. I wasn't ready for that. Not on the first date."

"So, what happened? Why do you look exasperated instead of satisfied?" Kara dangled her leg over the side of the chair and kicked her foot up and down as she waited for my story.

"Do you know Maddox Kingston?" I asked.

Kara arched one eyebrow. "Are you kidding? I helped build his brother's house up in the mountains. Those Kingston men." She closed her eyes as she sucked in a deep breath. "Hot doesn't begin to describe them. Even the dad is sexy as hell. He barely looks older than his sons."

I nodded. "Agreed, though I've only seen most of them in passing, except for Jury. So, we'd just sat down at the ice cream shop. Hadn't even had time to order. And Maddox comes barging in and *growled* at Harry."

Kara's jaw dropped. "You're joking."

"Not in the least. And the worst part was that Harry just sort of gulped, then he got up without another word and left!" Kara had the good sense to look completely shocked, at the time, I was completely shocked. "I haven't heard from him since, either."

It'd been several days since the horrible date. And I hadn't been thinking about it. Nope.

"So, Maddox then offers to drive me home, since my date abandoned me." I dropped my head onto the desk and banged it against my hand there. "I told him to shove it and walked home."

Her jaw dropped. "Why didn't you call me?"

I waved my hand at her. "I was wearing comfortable sandals and it's not a long walk at all."

"Wow." She stared at me. "I have no idea what to say."

"Neither did Abby," I said. I wasn't sure that Kara and Abby had met, but I'd mentioned my new friend to my old friend several times. "Except she said Maddox comes on strong but is a good guy." I rolled my eyes. "Good guys don't growl."

Kara shrugged. "I don't know. If one of the Kingston men turned their attention my way like that, they'd probably have to drive me home in a bucket." Her expression went soft. "'Cause I woulda melted."

I snorted. "Yeah, I get that." We both burst out laughing.

"Too bad they're all taken." She continued giggling. "Except Maddox, but it sounds like he's got a boner for ya." That caused even more laughter.

"Hey," I said when we'd calmed down. "If nothing else, it's flattering, right?"

She straightened up in her chair and wiped her eyes. "Yeah. Definitely. Are you going to see him again?"

That was a negatory. "Heck, no," I said with a frown which cemented my thoughts.

Kara laughed again at my vehemence. "Tell me how you really feel."

"Well, can you blame me?" I rolled back in my chair and crossed my arms. "He came across like a lunatic. I'm not planning to give him the time of day." Something about his behavior—the insanity of it, perhaps—rubbed me the wrong way. "No." He had to be nuts. Probably had an explosive temper, too. "Definitely not."

"You're saying no in a lot of different ways." Kara narrowed her eyes. "Are you trying to convince yourself?"

My jaw dropped. "No, of course not. I'm just saying how I feel, which is that Maddox Kingston is a wild card."

Kara cocked her head and grunted. I didn't respond, and she raised one eyebrow.

"Really!" I exclaimed. "I'm not convincing myself. I mean, sure, he's super hot. One of the hottest guys I've ever seen, actually." I hung my head back. "Certainly the hottest guy to ever be interested in me."

Kara grunted again, in a higher pitch.

"Stop that," I yelled. "Hot does not equal good for me or especially for *my daughter*."

Her face softened. "Okay, okay. I'll stop giving you a hard time about it. You're of course going to be extra protective of Tiffany."

My daughter was my priority. Always. There was never anything more important than keeping Tiffany safe. And someone who would be that irrational over someone they barely knew would surely get even more passionate with someone they knew and cared about. Like a child being super annoying. Or when she was older, disrespectful.

Best to not even go there.

"Tell me about this house." She sat up and we got serious. The next two hours were spent going over my measurements and pictures. All my notes ended up spread all over the desk as we discussed the potential investment versus the possible gain.

"I think this property would be a good one to flip and sell," she said. "Instead of rent."

"Why?" I asked.

She pulled my notes back out and pointed out a few places that were potential problems. "I have a bad feeling about the grade of the land in the listing." She pointed to the information on the printout from the realtor's website.

In the end, we decided this wasn't the best investment for my business. "It would be unethical to flip the house and not warn the new buyer about the potential problems that would be costly to fix."

Kara nodded. "You're a good person. It's refreshing to work with someone that values the right thing over the almighty dollar."

I neatened the papers and tried not to be proud of myself. "I just try to think about what my grandparents would've wanted with the opportunity they gave me. Screwing people over wouldn't have been a part of their plan."

My watch beeped and I tapped the screen. It was my mom. **Working late?**

"Oh, crap," I said. "I didn't realize how late it had gotten. Fill me in on the repair."

Kara ran over what she'd done at the tenant's house and we parted ways.

My parents kept Tiffany most days, though I was fortunate I could take her with me for many of my duties and responsibilities relating to my business. I'd asked Mom to keep her today because I wasn't sure of the condition of the property. Sometimes these homes listed so cheaply for flipping were very dirty or in bad enough shape it would've been dangerous for Tiffany.

My parents lived about twenty minutes away. I swung through a drive-through and grabbed dinner for me and Tiff. That way I didn't have to stop with my sweet girl in the car.

"Mom," I called. My father waved from his spot on the recliner. "Hey, Daddy."

"Pumpkin," he said without turning from the game. He'd become a couch potato since retiring. "Find a new house?"

I joined him in the living room for a minute, dropping a kiss on his half-bald head. "Nope. It's not in great shape."

"Well, I'm sure you'll get another soon." He patted my hand, but his attention was already taken by the game again.

"Mom!"

"In here," she called.

I followed the sound of her voice to the bathroom in her bedroom. She had Tiff in the tub. "Hey, babe. Bath time?"

"I had chocolate!" she exclaimed.

Mom gave me a sheepish grin from her spot beside the tub. "She had spaghetti for dinner, then chocolate ice cream. Her clothes are in the wash."

I laughed and shook my head. I should've asked before grabbing food. "Thanks, Mom."

"Well, you worked late again." She got that look on her face that told me she was about to scold me. "You work too much."

"Mom, I do not. Most of the time I take Tiff with me. I spend a lot of time with her."

Her exasperated sigh made my skin crawl. "I'm not talking about your parenting. You're a wonderful mother. I'm talking about dating. And *you* time. You need to carve out time to just be with yourself. And time to socialize."

"Mom. We've been over this a hundred times."

She waved her hand and grabbed the hand shower to rinse Tiff.

It didn't take long to get Tiff in a pair of pajamas—my parents loved buying clothes for her. She had an entire wardrobe at their house and her clothes constantly were in rotation between the two homes and two washing machines. I didn't mind. They loved doting on her. We said lots of goodbyes and gave lots of kisses. My father even managed to unglue himself from the game long enough to say goodbye to his sweet Tiff. A modern miracle.

"How was your day?" I asked as I drove us home.

My mini-me grinned at me in the rearview mirror. "Good!" She scratched her nose and a bit of her father shined through, a stab to my heart. I still missed him every single day. "We colored. And Nana let me play in the pool."

Mom always had a baby pool full of water and ready to play in the warmer months. "That sounds fun," I said with fake excitement.

As she rattled on about her day with her Nana and Papaw, I listened and encouraged her to talk and be expressive.

My heart pounded with love. Her father wasn't here to give her his, so I tried to show her twice as much affection. The car wreck that killed Kyle had taken my best friend from me. He'd only known I was pregnant with his child, the result of a drunken one-night stand between two lifelong friends, for a few weeks. I'd told him the moment I found out.

But he was gone, and she was here. And she was all I needed.

Chapter 2 - Maddox

"You guys can leave, you know," I grumbled.

Jury, Stefan, and Rico laughed, though Rico was subdued. He'd been quiet since coming to stay in Black Claw.

Jury and Stefan, not so much. They'd appeared at my doorstep a few hours before with a new racing game we'd all talked about wanting, as well as beer and pizza.

And there had been a lot of razzing me about my date. I was surprised it had taken them this long to get around to it, honestly. Especially with Jury's mate being Bethany's friend.

Jury looked around my living room. "When are you going to decorate?" he asked.

I shrugged. "Why? It's just a rental property."

Stefan handed me a fresh beer. "I have to agree with Jury. If you ever hope to change Bethany's mind, you're going to have to have a real place to take her, not this barely-even-a-bachelor pad."

Rico just shrugged when I looked at him to see his opinion. "I wouldn't decorate a rental either. But then, I would've just stayed with your grandparents. They're pretty chill."

Rico had Jury's old room at the big house. For the most part, they let him come and go, but nobody really ever forgot that the reason he was here was that he kept getting into trouble back with his clan. My great-grandfather's clan.

There were too many alphas in this family. Another reason I hadn't decorated. I wasn't sure I'd be staying in Black Claw, not that I'd told anyone that. There was no such thing as privacy in this small town. Even telling Jury, who was my best friend, was no guarantee that the secret would be kept.

The Kingstons were like royalty in Black Claw. It had been cool, at first. All the parties, all the girls. But it got old. I had a serious plan for my future, and it didn't include acting like a frat boy for the rest of my life. It had gotten worse since Jury was officially off the market.

"You know better than anyone what it's like to see your mate." I tried to defend myself. "And things might've been worse, because I could smell the desire coming off that creep."

Stefan sat back on my sofa and grinned. "I can sympathize. But I gotta go soon. Daddy-duties call."

I grinned at him. He hadn't stopped smiling since the baby was born.

Rico shook his head. "Hey," I said. "Don't be like that. As soon as these women figure out that you're here, you're a Kingston, and you're single, they're going to swarm. Maybe get the heat off of me."

Rico just shrugged. "I'm too fucked up in the head to worry about women at the moment," he said. "Even if a mate landed in my lap as they did for you assholes, I'd run for the hills. What the hell would I do with a mate?"

Jury and Stefan laughed. "Yeah, we thought the same thing, bud." Stefan finished his beer and grabbed another.

"I thought you had to go?" I asked.

He shrugged. "Harley is over at the salon. She'll drive home."

I was in no position to judge. I knew he didn't drink often, anyway.

"What are you going to do about Bethany?" Jury asked. He pulled the pizza box over and grabbed a slice, then held out the carton so I could grab one. I chewed a bite thoughtfully before answering.

"I have no idea."

Jury scoffed. "You took a long time for that bullshit answer."

"I don't know!" I exclaimed. "I barely know her, or even anything about her. I only know what you've told me, which is that she's Abby's friend and has a kid."

My mom was a single parent. She'd married a real asshole, too, which made both of us miserable. The only good thing that came of their marriage was my little sister, Hailey. "I'm in no position to be a stepdad. Besides, what would my mom say if she found out?"

Stefan shrugged. "You're twenty-two."

"Exactly," I said flatly. "I'm twenty-two. I'm not even out of school yet. And she has a *kid.*"

"Age is relative." Jury nodded as if he was some sort of sage imparter of wisdom. "It's about maturity, not years."

"Well, shit. I'm not mature enough to be a dad. Come on." I gestured to my bare apartment. "I haven't even decorated."

If I didn't stay in Black Claw, and I bonded with Bethany, she'd have to go with me wherever I went. She had a life here. No way she'd move away. The options were bonding with her then leaving her or giving up my dream. Neither option was something I was willing to consider.

"Man, take your time," Stefan said. "You know where Bethany is when you're ready. If you're fated mates, it'll keep. The bond isn't going anywhere. If you can stand to be apart, then do what you need to do to grow up, then seek her out."

He had a point. Dragons enjoyed very long lives. That meant that even if I took a few years to get my head on straight and finish school, Bethany and I would still have decades upon decades together. "What if she finds someone else?" I asked.

He shrugged. "That is a risk, sure. But she doesn't date much. According to Harley and Abby, that date you interrupted was the first she'd been on since before her daughter was born."

It wasn't right for me to be happy to hear that, but I was anyway. Even after nothing more than a few short interactions with Bethany, the thought of her on a date with another man caused Artemis to tense up inside me.

She will not find another man appealing now that she's met us.

"Artemis says now that she's met us, no other men will do," I said. "Is that true?"

All three of them looked pensive. I knew they were consulting with their dragons. Stefan was the first to nod. "Eros agrees."

"So does Nyx," Jury said.

"And Valor." Rico grunted. "Interesting. I never knew that. He says it's possible but unlikely that she could move on."

"Look what happened with my mom and dad," I pointed out.

Jury shook his head. "Yeah, but that was before Maverick had shifted the first time. I don't think the bond works before the first shift."

It does not work before the first shift.

"Artemis says you're right."

Jury nodded smugly. "See? Stefan's right. Take your time and do what you need to do."

We need our mate.

I sighed and ignored him. Even though it'd been several years since I first shifted and met Artemis, it was still really weird to have a voice in my head. It had taken me months to be able to jack off again, and Artemis had basically had to talk me into it.

I knew I should've been grateful at how my life had changed over the years. And I was grateful. I had a great life, away from my stepdad, I met and built a relationship with my real dad. Things were amazing here in Black Claw, they really were. But that didn't mean they weren't also suffocating.

But sometimes the whole dragon thing was too much. It was overwhelming at best. Some days I felt like I was going to drown in duty.

The rest of the night passed much the same way, going round and round about Bethany. Eventually, Harley called, and we walked Stefan across the street and down the block to the salon, then Rico crashed on my couch.

Jury went back to the house he rented with Abby. They were shacked up like a couple of newlyweds as soon as they decided to move in together.

The next morning, I got up and got ready for work, leaving Rico sawing logs on my couch. He really needed to figure his shit out, too. He was supposed to be in line for alpha, after our uncle Perry. At this rate, Rico would end up dead before he led Grandfather's territory.

I walked to the station, which was part of the allure of the townhouse. It was one street back from Main, so I walked everywhere. Almost like the benefits of living in the city, even though we were in the smallest town ever.

My dad pulled in as I turned into the parking lot and I met him at his cruiser. He got out of the car with a look on his face that made me groan. "What?" I said and turned away from him.

"Nothing."

Yeah, right. There was enough innuendo dripping from his voice to make my skin crawl.

"You got something to say?" I shot over my shoulder.

"Of course not," he replied. Dad put one hand on my shoulder. "Do you have something you'd like to tell me?"

I met his gaze to find his eyebrows lifted high enough to wrinkle his forehead. "I don't know, Dad, why don't you tell me when you turned into a gossiping old biddy?"

His face crumpled in mock pain and he clutched his chest. "Direct hit."

I rolled my eyes and went inside. Dad slung his arm around my neck and pressed a kiss to my hair. "I'm here if you need to talk, my boy."

Of course, he did this when we were inside the station, which was full. It looked like everyone was on duty.

"Aww," Axel said. "How sweet. Father and son bonding time."

I couldn't help the blush that worked up my neck. All the guys razzed me for a second but mostly went back to what they were doing. I headed toward the desk I shared with Carlos, who usually worked nights.

"Madd," Dad said.

"Yeah?"

"In all seriousness, come over for dinner and tell your mother before she finds out another way. It'll break her heart, you know that."

I sighed. "Yeah, okay."

My feeling of claustrophobia increased. I didn't even have time to process this whole thing before most of the town knew. Now I had to worry about my mom finding out.

All I wanted was to become a lawyer. I'd originally planned to go to a school a few towns over, in the city. Not too far from home.

But I'd been feeling so crowded, the letter in my bedside table started to look more and more attractive. A school in California, which I'd applied to on a whim, had accepted me. A very prestigious school with an amazing law program.

The more I considered it and the more this town tried to suffocate me, the better it looked. Nobody knew about the Cali school. Talk about Mom freaking out. If she found out I was considering going to a school several states over and thousands of miles away, the shit would really hit the fan.

I decided to keep it to myself for a while longer. I still had several weeks before the deadline for either school to accept or reject their admittance. I had to figure out if I could physically handle the California school. Was there even anywhere I could get away and shift? If not, the possibility of going out there went to nil. I had to be able to shift.

Artemis growled. He wanted me to find Bethany, claim her, and go to school here. Which was probably the smartest thing, considering I was a damn dragon shifter.

But still. I wasn't throwing out that acceptance letter yet.

Chapter 3 - Bethany

Invoice day was never fun. Thursdays were my office day. I balanced the books for the week, projected numbers for the next week and month, and followed up on miscellaneous office work and emails. It had been a productive day, though I still had a couple of hours before going to get Tiffany at my mom's. I hoped to finish up a proposal for Kara on a small remodel on one of my rental houses that we hadn't done much to when we flipped it. I had ideas for making it another Airbnb.

My phone rang, and I knew from the tone who it was. My shoulders sank and my heart pounded. I didn't know why I was surprised to see the number. A week barely went by without a phone call or sometimes two, and it had been nearly twice as long as normal since the last call. I sucked in a deep breath and tried to calm my twisted gut. "Hello?"

The drunk voice made me duck my head and put my hands over my eyes. "What reason did you have to turn him down? If you two hadn't argued..."

"It's done, Walter. It's over. There's no use going over and over what happened," I said.

The night I got the news was the worst of my entire life. As much as I loved them, it had been even worse than hearing my grandparents had died in a fire. Kyle had been my best friend in the world and the father of my only child. As soon as he'd found out I was pregnant, he'd proposed.

And I'd turned him down. For weeks we'd argued. He wanted us to become a couple, but I argued that the baby wasn't enough reason to take our relationship somewhere it had never been before. And as much as I loved him, and as happy as I was that we were having a baby together, the one night of sex hadn't changed my feelings for him. He was still my best friend and nothing more.

We'd had a particularly bad argument the night he died. He'd left my house and had been speeding on the steep, winding mountain roads. He'd lost control of his car and careened off a cliff.

His parents blamed me. They couldn't move past that initial deep hole of grief, not even for Tiffany. They'd come to the hospital the day she was born, and his mother had said she looked just like Kyle did at birth, broken down in tears, then handed Tiffany back to me and ran from the room. After that, I never heard a word from them. Not for holidays or birthdays.

Until about a year ago, the phone calls started. And they were always the same. Kyle's dad, after having one too many, called and reminded me that I was the reason his son was dead. It was my fault.

If only I'd been willing to provide Kyle's daughter a proper home by marrying Kyle, he never would've been angry, never would've driven like that.

The worst part about the phone calls was that Walter was right. I blamed myself just as harshly as he blamed me. But the difference was that I never could've ignored Tiffany. She was the light of my life and would've been the light of Kyle's. And could've been the light of his parents' lives if they could've seen past their pain.

I tried to tune Walter out, but words kept stabbing through my brain. Selfish, irresponsible, dead! Tears welled in my eyes. I dashed them away and sucked in a shaky breath.

"It should've been you!"

The line went dead. I wasn't sure why I took the calls. Guilt, probably. Guilt and grief. A therapist would have probably had a lot to say about it, but it was what it was. Walter needed to take it out on someone, and I was available. I didn't begrudge him his grief, even almost four years later.

It still hurt me every day. Every time I looked at Tiffany and knew she had to grow up without a father because we'd argued instead of talked. If I could've gone back and changed it all, I still would've told him no, but I wouldn't have lost my temper.

That night, I'd yelled. I'd told him he was my friend and that was all it would ever be. I'd cussed and told him to get it through his thick skull.

If I could've gone back, that's what I would've changed. The last thing I said to the best friend I'd ever had was, "For fuck's sake, Kyle! I'm not attracted to you!"

I stared at my phone for several minutes as the last words I'd said to him reverberated in my mind.

I couldn't remember the last thing he said to me. I'd never been able to remember.

After the phone call, I tried to focus on work, but it wasn't happening. There was no way I'd be able to get my mojo back. I never could on the days Walter called.

Damn it. I'd been in a great mood, too. Now that was totally ruined. I packed away the invoices and tidied up my workspace. I couldn't stand to come in the next day to yesterday's coffee and trash everywhere.

The day was only halfway over. I could've gone to get Tiff, but I didn't want my bad mood to spill over onto my sweet girl.

I ran upstairs to our living space above my office. One of the first things Kyle and I had done was renovate one of the homes so we could live upstairs and have an office downstairs. Now his bedroom was Tiffany's, but most of the house was the same. Memories of my friend were everywhere in the space.

I put on my hiking boots and pants to protect my legs from rogue roots and bushes, then headed to the car. There was a hiking trail that rarely had anyone else on it. It branched off of the main trail used by tourists going to see a spectacular waterfall, but they never took the path. It was too easy to miss.

It was their loss. There was a smaller but gorgeous waterfall along it as well. I drove straight there and wasted no time getting out of the car and on the trail.

Within a half-mile or so, I'd worked off a lot of my agitation. Sucking in a deep breath, I closed my eyes and walked a few feet after checking carefully to make sure the trail was clear ahead of me. Breathing in the forest, I moved slowly and listened to the sounds of the water, faint in the distance, sucked in my breath and enjoyed the scents of the blooming late spring flowers in the brush. I liked trying to connect with nature this way every once in a while. Without sight. Relying on my other senses.

The slightest sound made my eyes fly open. I looked around, but nothing seemed amiss. I kept my eyes open and continued through the forest. The late spring thaw made the air crisp and clean if a little bit chilly. The uphill walk had my blood pumping, so I didn't mind the slight nip in the air.

Another quarter mile up the trail, the sound of a branch cracking had me on high alert. Big animals tended to avoid these trails frequently walked by humans, but I was on one that was more ignored than others.

What had I been thinking? I hadn't told anyone where I was headed, and there could've been anything stalking me in the woods. We had all sorts of predators in Colorado. Big cats, black bears and grizzlies... Hell, we even had wolverines.

I stepped forward again but only made it about six feet before a larger limb snapped.

Nope. No, uh-uh. I whirled and hurried down the path the way I'd come. I had to get to a more populated place and hope that whatever was hiding from me in the trees would decide it was too dangerous to come after me.

My breath caught in my throat, sharp and panicked. I tried not to completely flip out, but it wasn't easy. Focusing on my breathing, I sucked air in and out as I watched the path, so I kept my footing.

My heart raced and ears buzzed as my mind filled with unlikely but possible scenarios about being attacked by a cougar and left for dead.

Oh, God. My daughter would've been an orphan. Her father already died tragically, that was going to be hard enough to explain the intricacies when she was older, but then my parents would have to tell her all about how her mother disappeared one day, never to be heard from again. They'd find my car days later, and search the mountains, but the cougar would've been too smart. He would've dragged me to some unknown—

"Hey!" Maddox stepped out of nowhere, directly into my path.

As much as I liked to think of myself as not a typical girly girl, my scream belied any of that. I shrieked at the top of my lungs and pumped the brakes, backpedaling and throwing out my arms. My hands slammed into his chest, but he didn't move an inch. I ended up plowing into him. It felt like slamming into a brick wall.

"It's just me," he cried with his arms around me. When I backed away, he released me immediately, but I couldn't ignore the heat from his hands as they steadied me, pressed against the small of my back.

"What are you doing?" I gasped.

"Calm down," he replied with his hands in the air. "You're okay."

"You scared the hell out of me!" I yelled. "Why didn't you announce yourself? Was that you back there, stepping on branches and shit?" I bent over and put my hands on my knees, trying to stop my pants from turning into hyperventilation.

"Not many people use this trail." At least he looked chagrined. "I'm sorry."

"I know," I said, still bent over. "That's why I like it."

I looked around. The parking lot was just visible. I'd made it to the part of the trail that was more heavily populated without even realizing it. "Did you come from the same direction I did?" I asked.

He nodded. "Yeah, I like to walk in the woods, off the trail. I was heading back this way." He indicated the parking lot. My car was the only one in sight. I started that way to see if maybe I was just at a bad angle to see his car. We stepped off the trail onto the asphalt. "Where's your car?" I asked, shooting Maddox a bit of side-eye. "Did you walk from the park?" The trail continued on, way down the mountain, and ended up in the city park behind Main Street.

He nodded. "Yeah, I enjoy a long walk."

I raised my eyebrows and moved slowly toward my car. "That's more than a long walk. Depending on how far you went up that trail, you might've walked over ten miles."

Maddox shrugged. "It helps me clear my head. Plus, it's good exercise." He shifted from foot to foot. His body seemed antsy. Was he nervous? This encounter was weird at best. Super-freaky was a better description. "Listen," he said. His shoulders tensed as he shoved his hands in his pockets.

"Yeah?" I couldn't help the suspicious tone in my voice.

"I'm really sorry I crashed your date the other night," he said. His gaze kept wandering around, but he landed on me.

"Really."

"Why'd you do it?" I'd been terribly curious. It hadn't made any sense whatsoever.

He sucked in a deep breath but kept my gaze. "I'd heard around the station that the guy you were on a date with had a history of being a tool and forcing himself on women. Nothing ever proved or stuck, but he's known around town."

My jaw dropped. "I don't get out much or get around to hear those sorts of rumors." His behavior at the ice cream shop suddenly didn't seem so insane. "I don't know what to say," I whispered.

He smiled. "You don't have to say anything. I should've explained this the other night, but the whole thing had me so angry and in my feelings, I didn't know what to say." He was right. He should've told me then, but I was glad he'd told me at all. "Thank you." I held out my hand to shake his. "I agree, you could've gone about it better, but I appreciate you looking out for me, more than I can describe."

As a single mom, I had to be so careful. And I'd had no idea about Harry. I could've found myself in a situation that I never would've truly recovered from. "Why can't you get anything on him?"

Maddox shrugged. "I'm not sure. I haven't gotten many more details. All I know is he's someone we watch." He scuffed his toe against the small rocks on the pavement. "Anyway, it was no big deal. It's my job."

"No, that wasn't," I said. "You could've just asked to speak with me privately, but instead you protected me fully and made it clear to Harry that he should leave me alone."

Some people would've considered that an overreach, but hell, I'd learned long ago that it really did take a village. I accepted help anywhere I could get it. If Harry would leave me alone because he was scared of Maddox, more's the better. That was one less thing I had to deal with.

My phone beeped in my pocket, reminding me I was back in service range again. I pulled it out and glanced to see a picture from my mom of Tiffany on the swing set. She had the sweetest smile. Mom sent me pictures all the time so that even when I was working and away from Tiffany, I didn't miss anything. I checked the time while I had my phone out. It had been long enough, and thanks to Maddox scaring the life out of me, I was over my rotten mood about Kyle's dad.

"Well, I thank you." I put my phone back in my pocket and smiled up at Maddox. "I'll let you continue on your walk. It's time for me to go get Tiffany."

He nodded. "Sure. Have a nice evening." I turned to leave, but his eyes were like weights on my back.

The Kingstons, man. I thought about them as I moved toward my car. They were an odd bunch. Everything anyone said about them was good. I'd never heard anything bad, outside of Jury and Maddox being playboys.

What family had nothing wrong with them at all, whatsoever? It wasn't normal. Everyone had something bad in their past.

Oh, well. They weren't my problem.

Chapter 4 - Maddox

My family had no idea that I flew in the woods surrounding the trail. Mostly because no one ever came there, and it was far enough away from home that no one could pick up on my thoughts when I shifted. I made sure to still go fly with them from time to time. They mostly just thought I didn't shift as often as they did.

Between hanging out here alone and going out with them, I probably spent more time in my dragon's skin than they did in theirs. It wasn't a competition, though.

She's scared of us.

Artemis was crazy. She seemed trusting and thankful.

She's scared.

I trusted his senses. If he said she was scared, there was a reason. After the disastrous way I'd handled her date, now showing up out of the blue on the trail? She probably thought I was a stalker.

It had been a complete coincidence though. I'd been in the middle of a shift and had barely gotten out of the way in time. I stayed well clear of the trails, normally, but I'd been flying through the trees, weaving in and out when I caught her scent. Artemis had turned and headed her way before I fully registered what I was smelling. He knew, though.

I reined him in at the last second and we landed in the forest not far from where Bethany walked on the trail. One of his back feet had stepped on a big branch, which was the crack that had sent her careening down the trail. I'd been half-sure I was mistaken about the scent until we spotted her with our own eyes.

The spicy aura had teased me on the trail several times before, but never fresh and in person like this. I hadn't put two and two together to realize that the tantalizing smell that had lingered in the air on several flights over the last year or so had been my mate.

Now I was positive.

Luckily, I'd figured out how to keep my clothes with me when I shifted. When I first found the trail and knew I wanted to be able to fly in this area, I'd made a very loose, elastic-handled bag and kept it on my back. When I shifted, it was still there, holding my clothes and cell phone. Artemis called it my dragon purse, no matter how many times I told him not to.

As soon as she took off running, thanks to Artemis being a blundering oaf, I shifted back to my skin and jerked my clothes on as fast as I could. Only my advanced speed and agility had made me able to overtake her even after taking the time to change my clothes. I probably should've just let her go and left her alone, but there was no way I could.

Once I knew she was nearby, I had to talk to her. Plus, Artemis had been agitated by the chase.

He loved a good chase, as any self-respecting dragon did.

After stepping out onto the trail, having her slam into my chest had been the highlight of my day.

By far.

Her scent had enveloped me, washing over me and igniting the urge to claim her as my mate, which of course I couldn't do. Just because she smelled like home and looked like a stone-cold fox didn't mean any of the problems had disappeared. We were still in the same predicament. She was a single mom with a successful business here in Black Claw, and I still needed to go to law school. Possibly very far away. That made everything such a mess. Why couldn't things be easy like it had been for Stefan, Jury, Axel, and my dad?

Now she was walking away from me again, almost to her car, and suddenly I couldn't stand to see her go. "Wait," I called.

She stopped and looked at me with a confused expression on her face. "What is it?" she asked.

"I was just thinking, maybe you shouldn't walk this deep in the forest by yourself." Any excuse to keep her talking to me ran through my mind, and this was the first thing that popped out of my mouth. How was I supposed to keep up this train of thought?

"What are you talking about?" she asked with a cocked head. I couldn't help but be distracted by the sunlight glinting off of the almost white highlights in her light blonde hair. Did she dye it? "Can you repeat what you just said to me?"

Her body language should've been my first clue to say never mind and walk away, but I'd never been particularly bright. "Yeah, of course. I mean, you were on a rarely used trail and on a weekday when there aren't as many hikers. It's not very smart. Did you even tell anyone where you were going?" She had to be intelligent, given how she'd built herself a business. She must not have been thinking about the possible ramifications of hiking alone. It wasn't like she had an inner dragon to protect her.

I hadn't meant to start chastising her, but the cop in me came out. Keeping people safe was my bread and butter. I had to think about safety, thinking ahead about possible scenarios of what could and probably would go wrong.

She put one hand on her hip. My second clue, but of course, I ignored it. "Not smart?" she asked.

"I mean, just not the best idea." It occurred to me that I was standing in the middle of a parking lot criticizing her. "There's no phone signal, you know." I tried to dial it back. Maybe I was laying it on too thick.

But her cheeks were already red, and her eyes flashed with an inner fire that was nothing like my own. "I'm fine." Her tone seemed cool enough. She looked a little mad, but not super pissed. She must have understood that I meant the advice from a good place. Bethany had a fairly level head, from what I could tell. She wouldn't jump to conclusions, thinking I was trying to come down on her.

"I'm sure you are," I said. "You know, though, there are bears and wildcats and stuff out here." Not that many in this area, truthfully. They all smelled the dragons and wolves and steered clear of our territory. "I just don't see you being the irresponsible type, with having a kid and all."

"This isn't the first time I've walked that trail and it won't be the last." She shut her mouth with a click of her jaw.

You really need to back off.

Artemis thought I was laying it on too thick. "I'm sorry," I said. "I'm not trying to be a jerk. Just thinking about safety.

It's part of the job. If you'd gotten hurt, and I hadn't been around, who knows how long you could have lain there before anyone came along to rescue you."

"What makes you think I need rescuing?" she asked. "I'm perfectly capable of taking care of myself."

I held my hands up again. "Of course you are. I don't doubt that. But there are dangers in these mountains that are bigger than us all." Including running into full-grown, fire-breathing dragons. To say the least. "At least stick to the more populated trails."

Her nostrils flared.

She's going to hate us.

"No, I'm not trying to tell you what to do," I said. I had to fix this. I began to realize that I'd taken totally the wrong tactic. "This all came out wrong. I'm just concerned for your safety." She blinked but didn't seem to get angrier, so

I kept going. "Think about your little girl. What would she do if something happened to her mom?"

That had been the final straw and far and away the wrong thing to say. Bethany's red face turned almost purple and her spine straightened, raising her to her full height.

"Let me tell you something, Maddox Kingston." She narrowed her eyes, and I felt like she was about to breathe lava over my face. Damn. "I don't need anyone telling me what I can and can't do. I don't know how old you are..." Her eyes raked up and down my body, but not in a sensual, fun way. More like she judged every immature molecule I had. Ouch. "My daughter is and *always* will be my first priority." Her upper lip curled as if I disgusted her, and thinking back over what I'd said, I deserved it. My information had been true, I wasn't wrong about the dangers. I really should've thought twice about how I said it to Bethany, though. She opened her mouth again. Damn, she wasn't done. "It's a fucking trail, meant for fucking walking. It wasn't like I was out rock climbing without a rope."

When she stopped talking, the silence deafened me with the weight of her anger. She whirled around and stalked away from me, but only got a few feet before pivoting on her heel and walking back, this time getting right up in my face. "You need to mind the business that pays you before you stick your nose somewhere that it's going to get cut off!" Once again, she stormed off. Her car door slam made me flinch.

Damn it. I'd been way too pushy. What was I thinking? She was a single mom! She was used to handling her own business her own way. I'd been so lucky she'd accepted my apology about the date, then I had to go and totally ruin everything.

I tried to warn you.

"Shut up," I growled in a quiet voice. She couldn't have possibly heard me as she backed out of the lot, but still, we could've been caught up here in the woods.

Bethany's tires barked as she threw the car into drive and gunned it down the winding mountain road. Damn it. I stared at her until she was out of sight.

If you'd handled that differently, we could've been riding back to town with her, surrounded by her scent and talking to her until she realized how much she likes us.

"I don't want to hear it," I grumbled as I crossed the road and stepped onto the trail that would lead to the park in town. Halfway down the trail, I cut across a clearing that had another unknown trail behind it. This one led to the Kingston property. I was supposed to go for dinner at the manor house with my grandparents, and thanks to my time with Bethany, I was late. I considered flying, but we'd already had one close call today. Best not make it more.

Walking would be fine. I'd get there soon enough. The next time I needed to get away and fly alone, away from my family, I'd have to be far more careful.

I had lots to think about on my walk, and when I stepped out into the backyard of the manor, I heard voices and smelled pretty much everyone I was related to that lived in town. It didn't matter that most of them had their own places, they always ended up gathered at the manor house.

The outside picnic tables were full of food. When we first moved back and started spending time in Black Claw, there had only been one table, which we'd all barely fit at. Now there were four, and all my uncles, aunts, and cousins were spread out, with the little ones running around the yard.

Grandma waved at me as she walked out of the back door of the manor. "There you are."

I headed to her first. "Quiet dinner, huh?" I'd been expecting a party of three. Me, Grandma, and Grandpa.

She chuckled. "You know I never can refuse any of you lot that want to come for dinner." She looked around and the love she held for all of us was apparent on her face. "It ended up being a family get-together."

After giving her a quick kiss on the cheek, I took the platter of macaroni and cheese from her and found a spot on one of the tables for it.

My mom stared at me from the table furthest out in the yard, close to where my little sister played with the babies.

Uh-oh. She knew something. I walked over to her and sat on the bench beside her, halfway lying on her. Any closer and I would've been in her lap. She laughed and wrapped her arms around me. I felt better instantly. I was a grown man, but something about a hug from Mom made all the difference in the world.

And just because she's my mom and knew me better than I knew himself sometimes, she leaned back and studied my face. "You okay?"

"Yes, of course." I was lying and I knew it, and she knew it, but I wasn't ready to spill everything yet. I was still stewing on it all. Plus, my entire family was around, and all the males had excellent hearing. I didn't feel like dealing with the fallout of them overhearing this particular conversation.

She gave me a look, clearly saying she wasn't buying it, but she didn't push. "I'm here when you're ready to talk."

I laid my head on her shoulder. "Thanks, Mom."

"It's okay for you to not be okay, you know?" She rubbed my back and I felt seven again. But in a good way. A safe way.

We sat at the table a long time with her arms around my shoulders and mine around her waist. I knew I was a lucky bastard to have my family. Guilt washed over me for thinking about leaving. Especially knowing what it'd do to Mom. But I couldn't live my life based on what made them happy. It had to be about what made me happy.

The thought of leaving them, especially my mom, made me feel sick, but there was so much going on in my head. And I had no idea what to do with it.

It didn't seem like the right time to tell her about Beth. Especially since Bethany probably had a bad taste in her mouth about me. Knowing Mom, she'd call Beth an idiot for not wanting me. But I really had fucked everything up, not that it mattered. Thinking about Mom telling Bethany off made me chuckle.

"What's funny?"

She smiled and waited for me to answer, but I just disentangled myself from her hug and kissed the top of her head.

"I love you, Mom."

"Love you, too, Maddy," she called. I walked over to the table full of food and started piling a plate full. I figured I'd tell her about Beth when there was actually something to tell. For now, I was going to save the whole fated mate conversation for another day. Besides, I was hungry, and Grandma's cooking was the best.

I just hoped nobody mentioned it to Mom before I did.

Chapter 5 - Bethany

"Well?" Kara and Abby stared at me across the table.

"Well, what?" I stirred my drink with the little straw, then sipped through it. It wasn't a sipping straw, it was a stirring straw, but I'd always liked using it to drink with.

"You've been way too quiet," Abby said. She sat beside Kara and they both stared at me like I'd grown an arm out of my forehead. "What's bothering you?"

I sighed. I didn't go out for drinks often. Maybe once every few months. The last time, I'd been here with Abby and that was the night I met Maddox. My parents had asked to take Tiffany for the night, and I'd gotten all caught up on my invoices, so when Kara suggested we hit the bar, I figured why not? I'd texted Abby and she'd been free too, and it had turned into girls' night. Abby and Kara had hit it off as soon as they met, so I knew it would go well. Except now they were both grilling me to talk about what was bothering me. "I had a run-in with Maddox."

Abby's eyes lit up with excitement, but Kara looked wary. "What happened?" Kara asked. "You don't look happy about it."

I'd been fuming since yesterday afternoon, and as soon as I started talking, all my anger and outrage came pouring out. "Maddox is a condescending dick, that's what happened."

Abby burst out laughing, but still, Kara looked concerned. She gave Abby a sidelong glance.

Abby just shrugged. "I know Maddox. He can be a condescending dick. But he's still a good guy. He just..." She pursed her lips. "Needs a little help figuring out some things sometimes."

"Like how to be a nice human?" I retorted.

Abby blanched. "Kinda?"

"Tell us what happened," Kara urged.

"I've never had to defend my parenting to anyone," I said. Except for Kyle's dad, but that was a whole different subject and not related at all. "He questioned my intelligence. He said hiking wasn't smart!"

Damn, my voice was shrill. How many of these drinks had I had? I looked at the glasses on the table. Yep, still on my first one. I was just that pissed. "I mean, how dare he? Who does he think he is?" For him to question me was frankly insulting.

Abby smiled, but it was a little pained. "I'm sure he didn't mean anything by it." She sipped her glass of wine. "He really is a sweet guy and though yeah, sometimes he can be a dick, most of the time he's not."

Kara shrugged. "You still haven't told us what happened."

I laughed and sat back in the booth. "You're right." I gave them a rundown of what happened out on the trail and tried to remember Maddox's words verbatim. "By the time I left, it was all I could do not to shove my fist down his throat," I concluded.

Kara sighed. "Yeah, that sounds pretty bad."

"Maybe he was just concerned?" Abby asked. "He is one of Black Claw's finest."

Kara chuckled. "He could've gone about this in a much better way."

"That seems to be his MO," I said. "Doing things wrong. I forgot to tell you that part." I launched into his explanation of why he'd crashed my date the other night.

Kara and Abby's jaws dropped as I spoke. "Harry?" Kara asked. "I've never heard that!"

"Me either, but apparently it's known."

Abby nodded. "I had heard it, actually. Jury mentioned it after it happened."

I fixed her with a level glare. "Why didn't you tell me?"

She shrugged. "You said he hadn't tried to contact you again. I figured if you mentioned another date, I'd warn you, but otherwise, I didn't want to upset you. I know if I'd gone on a date with a potential rapist, I'd be pretty damn upset."

That much was true. It had freaked me out. "I guess judging men isn't my strong suit," I said. "Too bad."

"Well, you should give Maddox the benefit of the doubt," Abby said. "I promise, he's a good guy."

I huffed and sucked the rest of my drink out of the glass. "He judged me. I hate feeling judged."

"And I get that, I do. I'm just saying don't let it totally color your opinion of him."

"Where's Tiff?" Kara asked.

"With my parents." They'd been thrilled to hear I was going out when I called to say goodnight to Tiffany. That was another thing making my mood sour. I hated how they thought I was wasting my life because I didn't have a man. I didn't need a husband to be happy.

It seemed like I was easily irritated lately, but really it was because everyone had been telling me how I should've been living my life.

A server walked past with a tray full of shots. "Hey," Abby called. "We'll take some of those."

She waved a few bills and the server smiled. "You got it. Girls' night?"

"Yep," Kara said. "We're ready to let go."

Abby paid her and Kara slid two shots in front of each of us. "Can you also have our server send us fresh drinks?" We'd all drained our first.

She nodded and walked away to tempt the other patrons with the rest of the shots.

"What is this?" I studied the amber liquid.

Kara knocked one of them back. "Oh, it's cinnamon."

My favorite. I grinned and held one up. Kara grabbed her second and Abby her first and we clinked the glasses, then all three drank. I followed it up with the second one but wanted more. Cinnamon whiskey was delicious.

"Why is it such a chore to drink eight glasses of water a day?" I waved the shot-lady down. I wanted two more. "But four shots and eight beers go down in no time?"

Kara laughed and got herself two more shots.

Abby hadn't taken her second one yet. "You might want to slow down a bit," she whispered. "Those things are potent."

I waved her off. "I don't drink often. What's wrong with having a good time? Besides..." I took my fourth shot. "It's girls' night!"

Kara high-fived me and our server returned with my Long Island, Abby's wine, and Kara's Sex on the Beach.

It didn't take long for the whiskey to set in. Kara and I hit the floor and headed over to the jukebox to find something we could dance to. As the first notes of the song we picked came over the bar's speakers, I whirled around, swinging my hips, and my gaze landed directly on Maddox.

Oh, great. Abby had just joined us on the dance floor, though she wasn't nearly as loose and comfortable as Kara and me. But then, she'd had half the shots we had. I didn't mind the drunk feeling. It was nice to relax.

I continued dancing around with Kara and Abby as Maddox and Jury ordered something at the bar. While they stood there, three different women approached Maddox.

None of them spoke more than a polite nod to Jury. The whole town knew he was with Abby, and the Kingstons had a reputation for being fiercely loyal to their women— once they settled down.

When they each had a bottle in their hands, they turned and scanned the room. I tried not to pay any attention to them, but it was hard to ignore them when they were headed our way.

Jury set his beer at our table and sidled up to Abby, wrapping his arms around her waist and moving close. "How drunk are you?" he called over the sound of the music.

She leaned in close and whispered something in his ear that made his face break out into a slow grin.

Ugh. I turned away from them, no desire to see them flirt and hang all over each other. They were freaking adorable, but I was drunk enough to let the envy show. So, better not to look. Being jealous of Abby wouldn't have made me a very good friend.

Unfortunately, when I turned away, it meant I looked directly at Maddox. Great.

"How are you?" he asked. He leaned against the wall near the jukebox, which put him in my bubble. Way too close.

I didn't answer. My glare was enough. Swirling my hips to the music, I turned away from him, but that put me looking at Abby and Jury, who were currently playing some sort of tonsil hockey. I kept going until I saw Kara. She winked at me and waved her arms to the music.

I mimicked her and we danced together for a while. In my drunken state of mind, somehow, I forgot that Maddox was right behind me. Dancing around, I turned and faced him again. Damn it.

"I owe you an apology," he called. His voice drifted over the music just loud enough so I could hear him.

"You're damn right!" I yelled. "And then some."

He held out his hand. I stopped dancing and stared at it. With a sigh, I gave in. I'd let him apologize, then go back to dancing.

Nodding toward our table, I ignored his hand and walked to the booth. He slid in beside me.

"My choice of words was terrible," he said. It was much easier to hear him here in the booth with the tall backs blocking some of the sounds.

"Well, thank you for apologizing," I said. I was about to tell him that I understood he was trying to be helpful and let it go, but then he kept talking.

"My words were true, but the delivery was all wrong."

Damn. He just kept digging his hole. Kara and Abby slid into the booth across from us, and Jury grabbed a chair to put at the end of the table as I tried to decide exactly what to say to the pompous asshole.

"It's a good thing you have a pretty face," I said. "Because your communication skills blow." I sipped my tea and soothed myself. He should've quit while he was ahead.

But he didn't look impressed by my words or particularly bothered. "You know, Bethany, in the time I've known you, I've put my foot in my mouth twice and said the wrong thing. But my intent was never to hurt you. Everything I've done has been with good intentions."

My jaw went slack and the little stirring straw fell out of my mouth and into the glass. "Excuse me?"

"Is this the type of person you are?" He looked at me like he never had in the time we'd known each other. "Do you take shots at someone to make you feel superior?"

My hackles rose. How dare he assume what type of person I was? He was the one that had been pushy, condescending, and overbearing every time we'd been around each other. He was right, though, I really had been trying to hit him where it hurt. My mind wouldn't move fast enough to formulate a defense and throw back at him how inappropriately he'd treated me.

"At least now I know I'm not missing out on anything," he muttered. He slid out of the booth and looked over at Kara and Abby. "Enjoy your night."

He left, leaving his beer on the table and walked to the door without a backward glance.

"Well," I huffed.

"Shit," Jury said. "I'll see you guys later." His chair scraped as he jumped up from the table to follow Maddox out the door. He leaned over and pressed a kiss to Abby's forehead. "I'll be back in a couple of hours to take you all home."

She nodded, then Kara and Abby watched him run after Maddox before both of them turned their gaze to me.

"What?" I asked.

Abby arched an eyebrow. "Was that necessary?"

"Do you remember what he said to me?" I asked. "Or are you forgetting how awful he was? The date? At the trail?"

"No, Bethany, you're in the wrong here. Maddox was trying to help. His heart was in the right place. Yours was not. You intentionally tried to hurt him."

I looked at Kara for backup. She didn't know Maddox and might have been more on my side.

Kara shrugged. "Sorry, Bethany. You were pretty harsh. He sounded like he was trying to apologize."

Well, fuck. So much for my fun night out. Now I felt like absolute shit. This entire night was one big reminder about why I tended to stick to myself. Mom life was the only life I needed. Every time I tried to do anything outside of just focusing on my daughter and my business, it turned into a disaster as this night had been.

I pulled out my phone and arranged for a rideshare on their app. It dinged immediately that there was someone already outside. In our small town, ridesharing programs were popular for the drivers but weren't all that used for the riders. The drivers liked to hang out at our only bar in hopes of picking up a rider. "I'm going to head home," I said. "This was enough excitement for one night."

"I'll come with you," Kara said. "You care if I crash at the office?"

"Sure," I muttered. "That's fine."

I nodded toward Abby. I wasn't mad at her, but she'd defended Maddox instead of me. Maybe I had been harsh, but after the things he'd said to me, I had a right to be. She was supposed to be my friend.

Chapter 6 - Maddox

Mondays were always dull at the station. It was nice when I was in school because I worked on homework during the boring times.

But I was between classes at the moment, so there was nothing but mundane Monday. I'd cleaned all the desks and had resorted to dusting all the legal volumes on the bookshelves. Again. I'd just dusted them the Monday before. And the Monday before that.

We didn't have a lot of crime in Black Claw. Even humans had some sort of sixth sense about them that made them steer clear. But officers were still needed, around the clock. Wrecks, accidents, and the small bit of crime we did have.

When the shelves were dusted, I sat at my desk and tried to pretend I wasn't thinking about my damn mate. I'd thought about her nonstop since Friday night when she'd basically told me I was an idiot with nothing more than a pretty face.

There was no way we were meant to be together. She was a total... well, she was a bitch! Our argument in the bar played in my head over and over, as it had all weekend. Like a movie that wouldn't stop playing on repeat.

I should've done things better, different. Said the right thing this time instead of fumbling through chastising her. But still, what she did crossed the line. It was one thing to argue or chastise me for being too condescending, but it was another to imply that I wasn't anything more than handsome.

Though, I had implied she was stupid for hiking in the woods alone. That had been bad. I probably shouldn't have done that. I hadn't meant to, but the damage was done.

In the middle of my hundredth replaying of the incident, the station phone rang. I snatched it up, fully expecting it to be something like a donation request or fender bender.

"Black Claw PD, this is Maddox," I said.

"Hey. Maddox. This is Elaine at county dispatch. We've got a public disturbance call that just came through."

That was definitely more than a fender bender. "Hit me with the details."

She rattled off the description and address. "I'll be right there."

Per protocol, I called Grandpa and forwarded the station calls to his cell. As sheriff, that was part of his job description.

I hung up as I got into the cruiser and headed toward the address. It wasn't far from the station, so it took me approximately three minutes to get to the scene. I radioed dispatch when I got there and turned toward the house. A neighbor stood in the yard across the street.

As soon as I stepped out of the cruiser, I knew where I was. I felt her, under my skin like a shiver down my spine. Biting back a groan, I walked toward the raised male voice I heard. The address was a well-kept home with a long driveway, and the sound of shouting came from the back yard. The neighbor hurried over. "Behind the house. I'm afraid he's going to hurt her. She's such a sweet girl." The older woman wrung her hands.

"Don't worry, ma'am. I'll take care of it." I took another moment to touch her shoulder reassuringly, then headed down the driveway.

Don't act rashly.

Ignoring Artemis, I rounded the corner of the house to see a man shouting at Bethany. She looked far more rational than she had the other night. I didn't like the person I met then.

She was drunk.

That didn't help her case at all.

"What's going on?" I asked in my deepest cop voice with my hands on my hips.

Bethany swung around to face me with shock on her face. "What the hell are *you* doing here?"

With my eyes on the guy standing way too close to my mate, I tried to make Artemis calm down and moved closer. "Got a call about a disturbance. Everything okay?"

She rolled her eyes. "It's fine. You can go."

"Well, once a complaint is made, I can't just go. What's going on?" I moved in, crowding probably closer than I would with any other suspect.

"This gentleman," Bethany said with steel in her voice, "is one of my tenants. I've notified him through certified mail that he was evicted and given him the ten days that are allowed by law. I actually extended it for a second ten days. He failed to pay his rent or remove his belongings, so I changed the locks. I will have someone come move his items to the front porch and lawn, as is outlined in the lease so that he can pick them up or they can be picked up by the city to take to the dump."

As she spoke, the tenant's face got redder and redder. If I didn't give him an opportunity to speak, he'd end up blowing anyway. "Sir? I need your name and ID, please."

He pulled out his wallet and handed me a driver's license. Andrew Hamilton. Like the president. No, wait, that was Alexander. Okay, then.

I studied the license and then handed it back to him. "Is this what happened, Mr. Hamilton?"

"Excuse me," Bethany said before he could speak. She held her hand up so he would wait. "I have no reason to lie."

Ignoring Bethany, I looked at the tenant. I wasn't asking him if he thought it was true because Bethany could've been lying. I asked him because that was protocol. Both parties had to be allowed to explain their side of the story.

"Sir," I repeated. "Did you fail to pay your rent even after Ms. Leeds gave you notice?"

The man puffed out his chest, but unfortunately for him, all it managed to do was stick his rotund stomach out. "Well, I've been a bit behind, but there was no reason that she had to change the locks. I could've caught up."

I nodded and refrained from exchanging a glance with Bethany. One sentence from the guy and I could tell he was a complete loser. Hell, I knew from the time I saw him, but whatever. I had to give him a chance to talk.

Just hit him with your fist.

Artemis knew I couldn't do that, but his possessiveness for Bethany made him a little irrational.

"So, you knew you could be evicted," I said.

"Well, I didn't think she'd actually do it." The pale man's cheeks reddened, and he glared at Bethany. "I mean, who only gives a man ten days to move?"

"I gave you more than twenty, and you're already two full months behind on your rent." Bethany wasn't taking a single ounce of his shit. "One more week and you'll be three months behind. I've been more than lenient."

"Yeah, right. A spoiled brat like you? You've got no idea what it's like to get behind, do you? Probably a trust fund baby."

"Enough." I fixed him with a glare. "It sounds like she went through the proper channels. If you want to dispute it, you have to go through the courts."

He opened his mouth to argue again, but I held up my hand. "I said enough. Showing up at someone's house—"

"Office," Bethany interrupted.

She stared me down when I shot her an exasperated look. "Showing up at someone's *office* isn't the way to solve any problems. Especially with an attitude like you've got."

His next words made my blood boil. "This bitch doesn't give a shit about life. Sometimes things get tough, but all she cares about is making her money."

I had to remind myself of my position.

Show him the error of his ways.

Artemis's idea was great, but I was the grandson of the sheriff. I was a deputized public servant of Black Claw. And I was one of the dragons that protected the town— even the less pleasant residents. "I suggest you rethink your choice of words," I said, struggling to keep my voice out of a growl. "This is a bad path for you to go down."

My chest burned as Artemis influenced me. The urge to shift was stronger than it had been the first few weeks after my transition. I wanted to wrap my arms around Bethany and tell her I'd never let anyone treat her like this again.

Instead, I sucked in a deep breath and watched the stupid man cower. Even though I hadn't said another word and hadn't been threatening, his instincts were to run screaming. He was pretty brave. He hadn't taken off yet. At least he had one personality trait in his favor.

"Fine." The sallow man looked about to stomp his foot. His nostrils flared and he looked back and forth between Bethany and me. "Can I ask, *please,* that you allow me to go get my stuff out?"

Bethany shook her head, but her face softened a little. "I promise, they will treat your items with the utmost respect." She pulled out her phone and pressed a few buttons. "Is your number still this?" She showed him her phone.

He nodded with murder in his eyes. "Yes," he said tightly.

"You have my word. The movers will pack and move your items with care. I'll text you as soon as I know the day and time they'll be available, but you can't go back on the property without a police escort."

"Officer," Andrew said with his neck stretched and his nose in the air. "Will you be able to escort me into the property if I'm missing any items?"

Hit him with your fist, then tell him no.

"Call the office the day before you're planning to go. We'll send someone out."

He pursed his lips and looked between us again. "Fine."

He turned and walked away. I expected him to go up the driveway, but he didn't. He went through the yard beside Bethany's. "Where's he going?" I asked.

"Most of my properties are on this street. I took the biggest house, then rented out the rest." She could've been a little grateful that I'd come to make sure the asshole didn't try to threaten her with violence. She just sounded irritated, though.

"That seems dangerous, having your tenants so close." I turned and looked up at the house. I hadn't paid a lot of attention to it before. We stood outside a French door, which was shut. "Your office?" I gestured toward the doors.

She nodded without replying.

"And you live above it?" I looked up at the windows above the French doors. A second level.

She sighed. "Yes. Tiffany and I live in the house upstairs. The basement is my office. Any more questions?"

I ignored her attitude. "Does this happen often?" I gestured toward the neighbor's yard. Andrew Hamilton was almost out of sight, two back yards away.

"No," she said. "Right now, I only have a handful of tenants. I screen them very carefully, and so far, they've all been amazing. He was too, for about a year. Lately, his payments were later and later, then they stopped coming entirely."

"Maybe you should think about hiring some security," I mused. Looking around the house, my mind whirled with possible upgrades she could do to make the home more secure. "You could use some floodlights," I said absently.

Bethany huffed, and when I looked back at her, she had her arms crossed. Damn it.

"No, wait," I said. "That's just a suggestion. It's none of my business." I backed away a few steps and held up my arms. "I'm not trying to overstep my bounds or tell you how to live your life."

She clenched her jaw, bringing my attention to her hair and the curve of her neck. The sunlight bounced off the blonde highlights in her hair. The urge to smell it was strong, but that would've been the height of creepy. She might've hired security to keep *me* away. "Okay, then." I clapped my hands together awkwardly. "I'll just head out, then. If you need anything, you know how to get a hold of me." Backing up a few more steps, I laughed nervously. "At the station."

She arched one eyebrow. I turned on my heel and walked toward the corner of the house, the weight of her gaze burning into me. No way I was turning around. Not only did I feel awkward, but I was also a little miffed. She could've been appreciative.

As I walked up the driveway, her response to my appearing to help her and make sure the dick didn't go nutso on her started to bother me more. I was only doing my job. If that was aggravating to her, I didn't know what else to do.

I didn't have anything against her, but she was obviously not a fan of mine. I'd gone about things stupidly, sure, but I tried to apologize, and even when working on the job, she could've been civil. Even just not rude would've been preferable.

At this point, it was clear that we were not compatible. I didn't know what the instinct thing was to make her my fated mate, or whatever, but it clearly was messed up. Faulty. There was no possible way we were meant for one another.

I was a lot of things, but intentionally hurtful wasn't one of them.

Not dealing with it seemed the best solution. I wasn't even sure I'd be in Black Claw that long. I'd just do my best to avoid talking to her. Maybe California was a good idea, after all.

The neighbor sat on her porch and she stood as I walked back to the cruiser. "It's all good," I called. "Thank you for your help." Interference, more like. Bethany hadn't wanted my help.

She nodded and walked in her house, so I slid into the cruiser and sucked in a deep breath. Time to head back to the station and turn the phones back on.

I went back and forth about Bethany the whole drive, with input from Artemis. He thought we should lock ourselves in a room with Bethany until we worked out our differences.

He was nuts. That would've only ended in one of us angrier.

When I pulled into the station, Dad's cruiser was already there. I walked in to find him at his desk, typing at his computer. "Hey, Dad," I said. "What are you doing here?"

He looked up and opened his mouth, then took one look at me and sat back. "I had some paperwork to finish. What's wrong?"

How did he always know? We hadn't even known each other for more than a handful of years, but somehow, he always read my face and body language. It had to be some sort of father-son dragon bond thing.

I sighed and sat across from his desk. "Dad?" I whispered.

He raised his eyebrows. "Yeah?"

"Are dragons ever wrong about their mates?" I sounded sullen and disappointed, and I knew it. But, fuck, I was sullen and disappointed, so it fit.

Dad looked stunned. "Somehow that isn't what I expected you to say." He shook his head and cocked his head. "I don't know, son. I don't think they're usually wrong. What does Artemis say?"

Artemis growled in response. *I'm not wrong.*

"He doesn't think he's wrong, but I do. I just can't, in any scenario, imagine her and me working together." I'd been over it a hundred times. The scenarios didn't add up.

"I've never heard of a dragon being wrong before," he said. "I know all of us have thought our mates incompatible at some point, but in the end, it always works out. I think Harley and Stefan had some incompatibilities like that, didn't they?"

I nodded. "So did Jury, but it worked out. This is different, though. She doesn't like me. At all. And she's not the same sort of person I am. She's kind of mean."

Dad laughed, but it sounded sad. "Sometimes people come across in ways they don't intend, then when you get to know them, you find they're not at all who you think they are. First impressions can be pretty rough."

He pressed a few buttons on the computer keyboard and shut the laptop. "Give it some more time. Maybe she'll surprise you, or you'll surprise yourself. And most of all, you have got to learn to trust Artemis. He won't lead you wrong. It's been my experience our dragons know far more than they let on to us."

I loved my dad. He normally had great advice. Finding him again had been the best thing that could've happened to me and Mom. But this time, he was far off the mark. Artemis just had some sort of obsession for her scent or something.

Putting some distance between us was the answer. It would help both Artemis and me get over whatever it was that made Bethany seem so attractive. She was a beautiful woman, sure, but there were lots of beautiful women in the world. She wasn't special.

I'd convince myself of that because Artemis was wrong. Bethany wasn't our fated mate.

Chapter 7 - Bethany

By the time Thursday rolled around, I'd had enough. Taking the rest of the week off seemed more and more attractive. Potential properties were nonexistent, my paperwork was caught up, and Kara had her maintenance that she didn't need any help from me to do.

I wasn't even sure she had any to do anyway. A tap on my office door was all it took for me to close my laptop and sigh. "Come in."

It was Kara. "I was just thinking about you," I said. "Do you have anything for me?"

She shook her head and plopped down. "No, after dealing with Andrew Hamilton's eviction yesterday, I'm taking the weekend off. I'll deal with any emergency calls if they come in."

I let my body go limp in the chair and hung my head back. "Andrew Hamilton was a nightmare. Thanks for your help with it. Anything happen I need to know?"

"Sure," she said. She'd gone over and supervised the movers to make sure nothing had gone wrong. "Andrew showed up with Jury Kingston and they walked through the house. Andrew pointed out places he said were damaged before he moved in, trying to make it so we have to give his damage deposit back."

I lifted my head and stared at her. "You're joking. Does he think he's getting it back? It goes to cover damages, sure, but it's already gone toward back rent owed."

She shrugged. "He seems unaware of that fact."

The urge to scream rose in my throat. "I put it in his lease agreement and eviction notice!"

Kara gave me a rueful smile. "He said something about you calling the police on him?"

That asshole. I'd given him chance after chance to make it right or try to catch up on his rent. He hadn't given me a penny in months. "No, I didn't. One of the neighbors did because he was screaming at me."

Her eyes went wide. "What? Why didn't you call me?"

I chuckled. Kara was so tough. In her line of work, she had to be. Talk about a male-dominated industry. "Maddox showed up."

She sat up straight. "No. What happened?"

I explained the encounter. The more I told her, the more she winced. "What did you say?" she asked after I finished explaining how he'd tried to tell me how to be secure, then backpedaled.

"Nothing," I said. "I stared at him until he went around the corner of the house, then went inside."

"After the bar, that had to have been awkward, but you may have been a little hard." She waited for my reply.

"How so? He keeps butting into my business," I said. "Every time I turn around, there he is."

Kara wasn't buying my excuse. "This time wasn't his fault. Someone called him, right?"

I nodded. My elderly neighbor had. "Yeah."

"Cut the guy some slack. He obviously has a thing for you." She shrugged. "He's so hot, he's probably not used to a female that doesn't fall all over him."

I snorted. "I bet you're right. He's hot and popular, but he's not smooth. I bet he's never had to be suave a day in his life."

We both lost ourselves to giggles for a few minutes. "Anyway, Andrew is out of my rental and our lives, thank goodness. And the Maddox thing was weird, but it's over now."

She shook her head. "I'm not so sure. I bet he'll try again."

"No way." I laughed and neatened up my desk. "He's got the picture now."

"Long weekend?" she asked and eyed my hands as they moved around the desk, cleaning up what little I'd been able to make myself work on.

"Yep. I'm going to find some fun stuff to do with Tiff and get my mind off all this. It's stress I don't need."

She grinned. "That sounds perfect. I'm taking one myself, provided nothing crazy happens." She blushed and ducked her head. "I've got a date."

My jaw dropped. "Why didn't you lead with that?" I asked. "Dish!"

She told me about meeting the guy at the hardware store in town. I didn't recognize his name. "If it goes well, I'll come over and share a glass of wine to tell you all about it."

I put my laptop in the drawer and stood, happy for her. Just because I didn't want to date didn't mean I wasn't excited for my friend. Kara was the sweetest and deserved a great guy who would treat her well. "Awesome. Let's get to it."

We said goodbye in the driveway and parted ways. She walked to the rental house she lived in, not far from the house Andrew had vacated. She got free rent; I got a super cheap maintenance person. It worked out great for us.

I hopped in my car and drove to my parents' house after shooting Mom a text to get Tiff ready. I wanted to start our weekend with a day at the park, then maybe we'd drive to the city tomorrow to their indoor pool. The season was definitely warming up, but not enough for outdoor swimming.

My parents' house was not the normal breath of fresh air. Mom had been on my case so much about dating and stuff that I dreaded what she might have to say when I went in.

"Hey, pumpkin." She was at the stove, stirring something for lunch. "Hungry? Tiffany is cleaning up an art project with Papaw."

"Sure, thanks." She dished out a bowl of her family-famous taco soup. "Oh, man. This smells amazing." I breathed it in and relaxed a little. She hadn't started about dating, so that was a good sign.

I relaxed too soon. The moment I had a bite in my mouth, she started in. "So, you're here early. Are you sure you don't want to leave Tiff? Maybe make a night of it?"

And here it came. "Mom, please," I mumbled. "Don't start." I swallowed my bite and glared at my mother.

"Well, do you have any dates lined up anytime soon?" She raised her eyebrows and plopped the spoon down on the stove. She was aggravated with me.

But damn it, I was aggravated with her. "Mom! Stop it. If I decide to date, you'll be the first to know. For now, I'm happy just as I am."

"Don't you want to find love? You're not getting younger, Bethany." She started with her mom voice. "Tiffany would benefit from a strong father figure, and you'd benefit from having someone to love and cherish you."

"I don't need a man!"

"Of course you don't *need* a man, darling. But trust me when I say it's much preferable to have a companion."

She sighed and put her hands on the island across from me. "Is it girls? Do you prefer women? Because that's fine, honey, I don't mind."

I glared at her.

"Really, if you're gay, just let me know. Your father and I discussed it and we're happy if you're happy." She looked so earnest and concerned that my irritation evaporated.

I burst out laughing. She was the biggest busybody, but I knew she only did it because she loved me. "Mom, I love you. It's not girls. I'm not gay. I'm content being alone for now."

Her face didn't reflect my humor. "I want more grandchildren, Bethany, and you're my only child. It's all on you."

I grimaced and finished my soup. She continued to rattle around the kitchen and go on about grandbabies and companionship. Ignoring her, I scrolled through one of my social media accounts.

"Are you listening to me?"

Mom's voice sounded irritated again. I jerked my face out of my phone and stared at her guiltily. "Sure, yeah."

"I said you're going to end up a crazy old cat lady."

Enough was enough. "Mother, if I decide to be a spinster, that is my problem. I know you are on my case out of a place of love, but enough is enough. It's time to stop."

She stared at me for a few seconds, but I didn't back down.

"Fine," she said. "I'll let it go."

"Thank you."

"For now."

I sighed, but it was the best I was going to get from her. She spent the rest of my visit talking about work, Dad, and Tiffany. The reprieve made me relax again. By the time we left, I wasn't irritated with her any longer and gave her a tight squeeze. "See you Monday."

She kissed my cheek. "Love you," she whispered.

After losing Kyle, I was so appreciative to still have both my parents in my life. Things could've been a lot worse.

I talked to Tiffany all the way to the park, then had to just about tie her down to get sunscreen on her before letting her go wild. She was only three but loved the slide. Since she navigated it well, I let her play here at this park that seemed more frequented by older children. Most looked eight or so.

We'd been there nearly an hour when a scream jerked my attention away from Tiffany. A little boy had fallen off the swing set. I jumped up, prepared to go help his mom if he was seriously hurt.

When he stood and walked away from the swings hand in hand with his mother, I relaxed and sat back down. Tiffany's shrill voice sent my heart into a stronger panic. "Mommy, help!"

I ran toward the jungle gym. "Where are you?" I called.

"The monkey bars. Help!"

How had she gotten all the way around there and on the monkey bars in the few seconds I was looking at the swings? I rounded the jungle gym to find her hanging off of one of the first bars. "How did you get up there?"

"I'm slipping!"

I darted forward, running as fast as I could over the sandy bottom of the play area. Like I had tunnel vision, I saw her hands slipping off the bars, one finger at a time. I wouldn't get to her in time. There shouldn't have been any possible way she could've gotten over here this fast.

Like a ghost appearing out of nowhere, Maddox darted under Tiffany and caught her just as she let go. He whirled her around, settling her into my arms as I ran up. I sat her on the ground and looked her over, but she was no worse for the wear, except for being scared. As soon as I was sure she was fine, I pulled her close and stood with her arms wrapped around my neck and her little sniffles in my ear.

"Thank you," I said in amazement. "Where did you come from?"

He pointed toward the trail. "I was running."

Belatedly, I realized he was covered in sweat. His moisture-wicking shirt was drenched, and he had beads of sweat all over his face. "How far did you run?"

It wasn't that hot out here. "Way up the mountain." He pointed in the direction that would lead to the trail he'd intercepted me on the week before.

He must've been running hard. "Thank you so much. I don't think I would've gotten to her in time. I know it's sand, but that's a long drop for a child as small as she is."

I pulled her arms from around my neck and looked into her tear-streaked face. "Honey, how did you get up there? You know you're not supposed to do the monkey bars by yourself."

She looked around the park. "A girl helped me get up, but I don't see her now."

I sighed. "This was why I always hesitated to bring her to this park and not the smaller one down the trail," I said. "But she loves the slide and most of the jungle gym is appropriate for her. I just keep her away from these monkey bars and the swings."

Maddox nodded and leaned in close to Tiffany. "Be careful or you'll give Mommy a heart attack." Tiffany nodded at him sagely, like she took his advice to heart. He chuckled. "Kids are crafty. They get into tough situations all the time. Don't beat yourself up. If you knew some of the things I did to my mom as a kid..."

I laughed. "I bet you did. You seem the type."

He put his hand over his heart. "Oh, what you must think of me."

His movements made my heart flutter, to my chagrin. This was the best, most natural interaction I'd had with him yet. Neither of us acted awkwardly or like there was some weight on us. "Well, thank y—"

"Is that the type of parenting that is supposed to keep our granddaughter safe?"

His voice burned through my good mood in a split second. I closed my eyes and sucked in a deep breath before I turned around to find Kyle's parents standing close by with their hands crossed and angry expressions on their faces.

I'd been worried they'd do this eventually. Barge in and try to make a mess of my life. "What are you doing here?" I asked.

They both ignored me. Tiffany had twisted in my arms to see who I was talking to. Of course, she looked just like Kyle and this was the first time they had seen her since the day she was born. They were stunned.

Kyle's mom, Mary, stepped forward. "She's precious," she whispered.

"I agree." I couldn't help the acid in my tone. "She's been precious for three years."

"Is this your idea of good parenting?" Walter asked. "Letting her fall off a jungle gym she had no business being on in the first place?"

My blood ran ice cold. "You have no right to judge anything I do with *my* daughter."

Mary sniffed. "We'll see about that." She shot me a venomous look but smiled at Tiffany. Too bad for her, Tiff saw the expression on Mary's face when she looked at me. Tiffany buried her face in my neck. "Mommy, go," she whispered.

"What do you mean, we'll see?" I asked.

Walter tugged on Mary's arm, so she stepped back beside him. "It means, this proves you're a negligent mother. You're too busy to be raising a little girl on your own. We've decided to sue for custody."

I looked at him in shock. After three years of nothing but drunken calls, he expected to get custody of his grandchild? "Over my dead body," I seethed. Moving to the side, I tried to walk past them, but Walter sidestepped and got in my way.

"You're a child playing house," he said. "And you killed our son. We'll get custody."

Tiffany was only three, but she was smart. She'd be able to figure out what they were saying, or at least their intention. "How dare you do this here, now? How did you even find us here?"

"When you weren't home, we drove by your mother's house," Mary said. "Your car wasn't there. Black Claw is a very small town. There were only a couple of other places you could've been."

They'd driven all over, looking for me. "You could've called, set up a meeting. Done this amicably. Now Tiffany is scared of you and you've made a scene in front of all these other kids." I gestured toward all the parents sitting on benches around the perimeter of the play area, shooting us looks and trying to listen in.

My anger began to build, and my voice shook. I opened my mouth to give them another dressing down, but a hand on my shoulder stopped me. I'd completely forgotten Maddox was behind me.

He stepped forward. "I'm Maddox. I may not look like it now, but I'm a deputy sheriff here in Black Claw. I think it would be best for you folks to leave instead of making threats."

"We have every right to be here," Walter sputtered. "We're Tiffany's grandparents."

"Be that as it may, lawyers exist for a reason." He looked down at me and Tiff. "In my professional opinion, you don't have a case, so you might want to back off with the threats before you get the consultation of someone knowledgeable in family custody cases."

"Who the hell do you think you are?" Walter hissed.

He smiled, but it was more threatening than reassuring. "Maddox Kingston," he said. He seemed to grow taller and more imposing, though of course, that was impossible. Suddenly having him around all the time didn't seem like the worst thing. I was grateful to have an ally against Kyle's parents.

They obviously knew the Kingston name. It carried more weight around town than I realized, though Kara had told me it did. Walter and Mary drew back slightly, and Mary smoothed her hair. Most of the time we'd talked, she'd only had eyes for Tiffany. More than likely, if I remembered her correctly, she had no interest in a custody case. She probably would've been happy with visiting Tiff.

Walter was another story. But he grunted and looked at Mary. "We'll consult an attorney, then." He shot me one last glare, then he turned Mary around with one hand on the small of her back. He was so damn controlling. It was a big reason we'd always spent time at my parents' house as kids instead of Kyle's. He didn't want me exposed to his Dad's vitriol.

We watched them walk away, and my adrenaline left as soon as their car pulled out of the parking lot, leaving me shaking. Tiffany brightened up, with the resilience only a toddler could have. "Mommy, slide?"

"Sure, sweetie. Go slide."

Maddox's hand was still on my shoulder. It slipped off when I bent down to set Tiffany on the sand and watched her run toward the steps. "Everything will be okay," he said. "You've got a great reputation, and everyone in Black Claw knows how devoted you are to your daughter."

I didn't take my eyes off of my daughter after she almost fell, but his words warmed me and helped me calm down.

"I am a good mother," I whispered defensively. "I'm not good at many things, but I'm a damn good mom."

He put his hands on my shoulders again and squeezed. I didn't mind the touch or the comfort, so I didn't step away. This was a new leaf in our relationship and how we treated one another.

I wasn't mad at it.

"Everything will be okay," he whispered.

I didn't know why his words settled my gut and nerves, but they did. I believed him. Turning so that I could swing my head back and forth and look at Maddox and Tiffany, I smiled at him. Then I quickly found my daughter in the jungle gym again. "Thank you."

"Call me if they follow through on their threats," he said. "I'm going to college to be a lawyer and know all the lawyers in the county through my work at the police station. I'd be happy to help you find someone."

I watched him walk away after thanking him again. He called goodbye to Tiffany, then got back on the trail and broke into a jog. I found Tiffany again and watched her with an eagle eye. In the back of my mind, I began questioning my sanity and whether I'd pushed away a good man.

Chapter 8 - Maddox

"So then, Carrie told Cassie that Connie and Callie were doing cheer routines behind her back, can you believe it?"

I stared at my sister, Hailey, in amazement. "All these people are real, with virtually the same name?"

She dissolved into giggles and threw herself against the couch. "Madd, you're so crazy. Of course they're real, they're my best friends in the whole world!"

As she chattered on, I watched her animated face and marveled at the fact that she was already thirteen. She was gorgeous with nearly black hair and big eyes. She looked more and more like our mom every day. And thankfully nothing like her biological father. She loved sports and was a tomboy, but one day I had a bad feeling I'd have to turn into the protective older brother when she started dating and went through puberty and all that.

Ugh. I hated the thought of my sweet little sister being old enough to date. But my dad was so protective of his stepdaughter, I probably wouldn't have gotten a chance to be her protector. He'd likely take care of it.

I caught a boy's name in her chatter. "Wait, go back," I interrupted. She cocked her head and looked at me with all the attitude she could muster. "Who is the boy?"

Hailey rolled her eyes. "He's just a boy," she said. "I don't have time for boyfriends, so don't go there *again.*"

Maybe I'd lectured her once or twice about the untrustworthiness of teenage boys. Or three times. It was my job as her brother, after all. "Fine," I said.

"Come eat!" Mom yelled from the kitchen. We walked in to find Dad already at the table and my favorite dinner spread out. Taco salad.

I groaned and plopped down. "This looks great."

"Why don't you come to eat with us more often?" Mom asked. "I know all you're eating in that little apartment is frozen dinners."

Pausing in the act of filling my bowl, I shot her a fake-haughty look. "No. I also get takeout."

Hailey burst out laughing and Mom pushed at her head. "Don't encourage him."

"Oh, Madd, I meant to ask." Hailey grabbed a bowl and took the spoon from me. "What happened at the park the other day?"

I furrowed my brow and stared at my little sister. "Thirteen-year-olds gossip too much. How'd you even hear about that?"

"Cassie's older sister was babysitting and took her along to help. She said you were a hero."

I rolled my eyes at her and swallowed a big bite of salad. "I was in the right place at the right time."

Hailey shook her head. "Cassie wouldn't lie."

"What is she talking about?" Mom asked.

"I was running on the trail behind the park and came out of the woods in time to see Tiffany Leeds about to fall off the monkey bars. Everyone had their eyes on her, so I put a little extra speed in my run while they weren't looking and caught her before she hit the ground."

Mom raised her eyebrows. "Bethany's daughter?"

I nodded. "You know her?"

"Yeah. She's friends with Harley and Abby. We've met at the salon. She's a sweet girl." She handed napkins out to everyone, and as usual hadn't even sat down yet to eat her own food.

Dad hated it when she did that, so he jumped up and got her a drink and nudged her toward the table.

"Well, it was a lucky coincidence I was there. Not a big deal. Good thing, though. She's so little. I bet she would've broken something if she'd fallen."

I was equally glad I'd been there to stand next to Bethany when Tiffany's grandparents showed up. She probably would have handled it on her own, but me being there seemed to have made it a little easier for her. As much as I didn't care for her or her attitude, she was a good mother. Everyone that knew her could tell that. I didn't know the whole story with her ex, but she didn't deserve whatever that was about.

"Well, I also heard you went on a date with Bethany," Hailey said haughtily. She tossed her dark hair over her shoulder. Dad choked on his iced tea and Mom stared at me with her eyebrows up.

Damn it, Hailey. "You're too sassy for your own good," I said. "Don't you know gossiping is bad?"

Hailey took a dainty bite. "It's not gossip if it's true."

Mom turned her glare from me to my sister and arched an eyebrow. "We'll talk about gossiping later, miss."

Hailey shrank a little under Mom's scowl, but then she turned it back to me. "What is she talking about now? Start talking."

"I told you to tell her," Dad muttered, his face close to his bowl.

"Tell me what?" Mom looked like she was getting upset.

I groaned and stuffed a huge bite in my mouth, then looked at Mom as I chewed with the most innocent face I could muster.

Mom's face went from curious to upset. Then, it darkened, and her eyebrows fell. "Do not tell me she's your mate."

I didn't know why she hated the idea so much. I didn't think Bethany was right for me, but she wasn't *that* bad. I was surprised to feel defensive of her, even after deciding Artemis was wrong about her being my mate.

"Artemis thinks she is," I said when I finally swallowed. "But I'm not so sure."

She was silent for far too long. I got in three big bites before she spoke again. "Dating a single mother isn't going to be easy."

Ugh. Here we went with the lecture. "I know, Mom. I have no current plans to date her, anyway."

Mom sniffed. "That will change. If Artemis recognizes her as your mate, you won't be able to stop yourself."

I met her gaze and saw the truth in her face. She believed it to be true, anyway. "We're not compatible."

She waved her hand, ignoring her food, and continued as if I hadn't spoken. "You need to be prepared to be a father. You can't just give it a shot then walk away. That doesn't work for fated mates or children, either one."

She carried on talking about the importance of raising a child, especially one that wasn't biologically mine. Dad nodded along as she spoke and winked at Hailey a few times. She just rolled her eyes. Mom wouldn't let anyone get a word in edgewise, anyway. When she went on a rant like this, we all knew to just let her vent her spleen and get it out of her system.

As soon as she stopped to take a breath, I jumped in. "I know, Mom. I know. I'm aware of everything you're saying. But we're not a good match. Bethany isn't the sort of person I expected to spend the rest of my life with. And besides, she doesn't seem to care for me at all."

That was the wrong thing to say. Damn it.

"What do you mean? Why doesn't she like you?" She pointed her fork at me and wiggled it a little, enunciating her words. "You're handsome, smart, come from a good family. What more could she want? You'll be an excellent father, too." She clanked her fork down in her bowl of uneaten taco salad and huffed. "Not to mention you're going to be a lawyer. Even if your father's family didn't have money, you'd be able to provide for a family."

I didn't butt in to tell her Bethany probably didn't need my money, anyway. She had a successful business that she seemed to care about. That was a point in her favor, anyway. At least we could be sure she wasn't a gold digger.

When she wound down her rant, she sighed and grabbed my hand across the table. "Promise me you won't rush into anything you're not ready for."

"I won't, Mom. I promise."

It's obvious she was nervous about the whole thing. But she sighed. "It's hard for me not to want to interfere. You're still my baby boy in my heart. I want to rush in and try to fix everything for you."

At this point, I would've gladly let her. "I know, and I appreciate it."

Hailey rolled her eyes. "It's a girl. It's not brain surgery."

I snorted and ruffled her hair, which set her off screeching to the bathroom to fix it. "Yeah, right. Wait till it's her turn."

It was Dad's turn for his face to darken. "Let's not."

The rest of the dinner passed in relative comfort. When it was time to go, I grabbed Mom's arm and pulled her into a hug. "I'll always be your baby, Mom."

She laughed in my chest. "My baby who's twice my size or more."

I squeezed her tight until she squeaked. "That's okay. You can still want to protect me."

It was nice to have her arms around me. It felt like when I was little and hugging my mommy was the cure for most problems.

After pressing a kiss to her head, I walked out to the truck Dad gave me when I first moved to Black Claw. I'd taken care of it. It had several upgrades since I first got it, and I kept it in the garage at the house most of the time. My legs worked fine for most errands.

I'd told Jury I'd meet up with him for a beer after dinner with my parents. His mate, Abby, was doing some girls' thing with Harley and maybe Bethany.

As usual, as soon as I walked into the bar, one woman after another interrupted my walk across the floor toward Jury. It would've been flattering if the women weren't so obvious. I made it to the table, and we couldn't even take a sip of our beers before another woman came up. It was particularly worse tonight because Rico was in the booth beside Jury, with Jury on the inside. Every other woman touched his arm or mine flirtatiously. Every time one of them put a hand on me, Bethany's face flashed through my mind.

I didn't even want to be her mate and already I felt like I was being unfaithful just by being near a flirtatious woman. Normally I might've encouraged one of them to come home with me for a one-night stand, but the idea was repugnant.

Because you have a mate.

Artemis was right. She was my mate, even if it wasn't going to work between us. Did that mean I couldn't ever date another woman? Like... ever?

"Is this normal?" Rico asked. Jury had finally convinced himself to stop punishing himself for a night and come hang out with us.

"Yes," I said sullenly. Jury said the same word at the same time, causing all three of us to chuckle as another woman walked up and offered to buy Rico a drink.

He smiled politely and shook his head. "I'm good, but thank you."

She nodded, looking a little disappointed, but walked away.

I felt the pull before she even entered. My gut clenched and I couldn't stop my head from swiveling to watch the door. Bethany walked in with her blonde hair in a messy bun. She didn't have on any makeup, and she wore yoga pants and a big T-shirt.

What in the world was she doing here?

And why did she look so incredibly sexy like that? Normally I gravitated toward women fully made up and in nice clothes. It proved they took care of themselves.

She looked around, and in seconds, her face hardened, and she made a beeline for the opposite side of the room.

A big guy stood from a table when he saw her. He looked about my age, and as soon as he was on his feet, it was painfully obvious that he was fall-down drunk. I focused on her lips and channeled a little extra energy into my ears to make out what she was saying. Her words reached me like through a tunnel. "You know how stupid it is for you to get this drunk." She put her hand on his arm, but he was a big guy. He jerked away and said something unintelligible.

"Come on, Nash. Let's go." Bethany sounded exasperated. Nash turned his back to me, so I couldn't really make out his response, but his body language said he had no intention of leaving with her.

"Be right back," I muttered. It took me seconds to cross the bar floor. "Bethany, are you okay?"

She looked at me in surprise. "What are you doing here?"

I gestured to our table. "Out with Jury and Rico."

She looked over and nodded at them. The big guy turned back to the table and grabbed a beer. A girl I didn't know glared at him. "That's mine."

He shrugged and drank it anyway.

"You're always coming to my rescue," Bethany said as she grabbed the guy's arm again. "Come on, Nash!"

He shook her off again.

"Hey," I said in my best cop voice. I let Artemis add a bit of alpha weight to it as well. The guy, Nash, turned toward me in surprise. "Time to go."

For a second, I thought he was going to argue with me. But he sighed. "Fine."

Bethany followed close behind, then darted around him and opened the door. The big oaf had looked like he was going to plow right through it.

I stayed behind him in case he decided to turn around, but once he'd made up his mind to leave, he didn't give her any trouble. She opened her passenger car door and I watched in amusement as the tall man folded himself down to sit in

Bethany's small car. He looked like a busted can of biscuits in it.

"Thank you," she said when she shut the door on him.

"I can follow you," I offered, but she waved me off.

"No, it's okay. He's my cousin. He drunk texted me, and I called and realized how wasted he was. He's always gotten into trouble, but I thought maybe I could prevent it this time." She looked into her car and laughed. "He's already passed out."

"It seems like you've done this before."

She sighed. "Yeah. A time or two. Or more."

"Reminds me of my cousin, Rico. He's living with my grandparents. They're trying to help him get his head on straight."

"I do thank you for helping," she said softly.

Ducking my head, I shrugged. "It's my job."

Bethany studied my face for a moment. "It was more than that, and I appreciate it."

She smiled softly and walked around her car. I waved as she got in, but after she turned the engine on, she rolled the window down. "Maddox," she called.

I hurried around the car. "Yeah?"

"Would you like to try again?"

"What do you mean?" My stomach danced with anticipation because I had an idea of what she meant.

"Let's go to dinner." The brake lights shone behind the car as she put it in reverse, but she didn't move yet.

I stared at her in shock until she raised her eyebrows. "We don't have to?"

"No," I cried out. "I mean, yes. Sure, yeah. I'm off this weekend. Dinner. Tomorrow?"

She smiled again and backed out of the parking spot.

I stood in the parking lot in stunned silence as she drove away with her cousin in the passenger seat.

I had a date.

Chapter 9 - Bethany

"Don't let him pay," Mom said as I kneeled near Tiffany. "He'll think you owe him something."

I sighed and ignored her. She'd been throwing dating advice at me since I arrived with Tiff. She'd kept her last night so I could do facials and manicures with Abby and Harley, so I hadn't planned on leaving Tiff a second night in a row, but the urge to ask Maddox to have dinner had overwhelmed me, and I'd given in to it. Like an idiot.

More than likely, he'd say or do something to ruin everything. Again.

"Mom, stop," I said, and hugged my daughter.

My mother's excitement was palpable in the air. She was so eager to marry me off. "If the first few dates go well, then you can get excited, okay?"

I plopped Tiffany on my Dad's lap and he grabbed the TV remote. "I got you a new movie," he said.

Tiff's face lit up. "The one with the ice princesses?"

He nodded, and I groaned. "I've been avoiding that one. The little girls are obsessed with it."

"Pshaw," he said. "Let her enjoy it."

It wasn't about her enjoying it. It was about me distinctly not enjoying it. But, of course, I'd let her become obsessed with it if that's what she wanted. "Sure, Daddy." I dropped a kiss on his head and headed for the door.

At the last minute, after I said goodbye to my mother, who was still bursting with excitement, Tiffany called out my name. "Mommy, wait!" She jumped off my dad's lap and hurried across the room. "I need another hug."

I nearly canceled the date right then. "Are you okay?" I bent over and gathered her into my arms.

"Yes." She squeezed my neck with her strong little arms. "I just needed another hug."

"Tomorrow we'll spend the day together, okay?" I whispered in her ear. "And do something fun."

My mother sniffed and held out her hands. "Come on, sweetheart. Let's go see if I've got some cookies in the pantry."

Tiffany brightened up and lunged for her grandmother. "Don't expect the worst," Mom said. She couldn't resist a bit more advice. "Just relax and try to have fun." Mom winked as I slipped out the door. "Let things happen naturally," she called.

I yanked the door shut before she could think of any more advice, then hurried to my car. Suddenly, now that it was time to drive to the only restaurant in town that could be considered a nice date night, I was nervous. I wanted to do exactly as my mom had said and let things progress naturally, but it wasn't easy.

It was just dinner. No big deal, no strings attached. Just two people eating to see if we could start a conversation without arguing or saying the wrong thing. There was no reason for the butterflies in my stomach.

I pulled into the restaurant's parking lot far too quickly. I was a good fifteen minutes early, but I spotted Maddox standing outside the restaurant's front door as soon as I parked.

He hadn't seen me yet, I didn't think, so I grabbed my purse and checked my hair and makeup. I wasn't one to wear a face full or try all that contouring stuff people did these days. Just the thought of trying to contour my makeup made me nervous.

I had on a light layer of base, a brush of lavender shadow in my crease, and mascara. At the last second, I dabbed on a neutral lip gloss, tossed my blonde hair around a little, and stared at the restaurant.

"It's no big deal," I whispered. "Just dinner."

Steeling my nerves, I made myself get out of the car. As soon as I stood, Maddox's gaze darted toward me and glued to mine.

Walking toward the front, I had to make myself stop staring. I was about ready to drool. He wore a snug button-down shirt that accentuated his muscles. And he had the sleeves rolled up to just underneath his elbows. Why was that so hot on a guy?

And how had I been able to ignore how buff he was? I mean, I'd known he was attractive, but his shirt and crisp slacks accentuated what a perfect body he had.

I thought about the few stretch marks remaining around my belly button from having Tiffany. They were my tiger stripes, and I tried to be proud of them. But would a man like that want me with my imperfections?

Maddox stared at me as I stepped onto the sidewalk beside him. He shook his head and grinned. "You look amazing."

I looked down at my dress and feigned modesty. I'd tried on what felt like a million outfits before settling on an LBD. "Oh, thank you. You look nice as well." What an understatement. He looked like a million bucks, easily.

Maddox held the door open and when we went in, the hostess nodded at Maddox and led us past the people waiting in the lobby. He put his hand on the small of my back and I said a prayer of thanks that I'd worn the bra with light padding. As soon as he touched me, my nipples hardened like rock candy ready for a lick. "I came early and put our names down," he whispered. "And greased her palm a little."

I tried not to shiver, and Maddox kept his hand on my back the entire walk to the table. Normally, I might've seen that as slightly chauvinistic, but when Maddox did it, it just made me horny. Great.

The hostess seated us at a small table right by the huge windows that made up the back wall of the restaurant. They were treated somehow so the glare of the restaurant didn't obstruct our view of the mountains and moonlight. "It's beautiful," I said. "This is pretty much the only date restaurant in a half-hour drive, but I never mind."

"Neither do I," he agreed. "The food is excellent, and I could watch this view all day."

We slipped into a slightly awkward silence. The server came and dropped off goblets of ice water and took our drink orders. We both laughed softly when we each ordered iced tea.

The uncomfortable silence stretched through our menu selections, though we did each say a few lines about what we were going to have. When the server came and took our orders and left with the menus, I sighed. "I'm sorry," I said bluntly. "I can be harsh sometimes. When I feel cornered, it would be fair to say I can get nasty." I ducked my head and battled guilt for my previous behavior. "We got off on the wrong foot, and it wasn't your fault for putting your foot in your mouth. It was mine for responding rudely. You didn't deserve my hostility."

Maddox smiled at me. "I appreciate your apology, but I deserve a little bit of the blame, at least. I was condescending. I found myself overwhelmingly attracted to you and it was like I couldn't say the right thing. I didn't mean to come off like I knew what was best for you or how you live your life." He took a sip of his water. "Most of all, I want you to know that I'm absolutely positive that you're a good mother. I didn't mean to imply otherwise."

His apology soothed the last of my worry about our date. The rest of the night went smoothly, to my delight.

"Tell me about yourself," I said while we waited for our food.

"Well, I have a bachelor's degree in criminal justice, and I've been accepted to law school."

I couldn't keep my surprise off my face. "I just assumed you were going to be a cop," I said. "That's wonderful."

He shook his head. "I see why you'd think that, but I'm technically only part-time at the Black Claw PD."

The server dropped off our plates, so we spent a few minutes digging in. I moaned in delight. "I love this chicken piccata. Want to try it?"

He nodded eagerly, so I cut off a piece and slipped it onto his plate. "Bite of my steak?" he asked.

"Sure," I said. "I'm a huge steak fan."

As soon as he stuck a chunk of his meat out on his fork, I recoiled. "Sorry," I said. "I'm not a big fan of *rare* steak."

Maddox sat back and gave me an appraising look. "So you like beef jerky, not steak?"

"No, it's just that I like to do more than walk my steak past the grill," I teased.

Things flowed so easily after that I found myself telling him about Kyle. I didn't know why I'd been so resistant to getting to know him. He was a great listener, and very sympathetic about what I'd gone through with Kyle, then he was very interested in my business and how I'd grown it.

After that, he asked me about Tiffany and what it had been like having her without Kyle. He smiled as I spoke. "What?"

"Nothing, it's just sweet the way you light up when you talk about your daughter."

Of course, that made me blush even more. But he wasn't done.

"I feel like you love Tiffany the way my mom loves me, and that's a pretty powerful thing."

Knowing he had such a good relationship with his mother was a good sign. And I knew he lived in an apartment by himself, which meant his relationship with his mom wasn't *too* good.

"How do you feel about kids?" I asked.

He paused and looked down at his half-eaten steak. "I don't have any immediate plans," he said. "Having a child right now would definitely throw a kink in the works as far as going to law school."

At least he was honest with me.

"I do want kids one day, though," he said. "For sure."

So, was there any point to continuing this attraction and flirtation we had with each other? He didn't want kids yet, and I had one. The ultimate downfall of single parent dating.

"I don't think things are serious enough at this point that we need to worry, are they?" he asked. "We're just having dinner and trying to become friends instead of being aggravated at each other."

I nodded. "I can agree with that. I'd never pressure you into something you weren't ready for. And you're right. It's nice to have a date, especially with no obligations."

We moved on after that, though knowing he didn't want kids yet left a slightly sour taste in my mouth.

By the time our dessert came, I was comfortable enough to ask him a potentially embarrassing question. "Why do women fall all over you?"

Maddox stared at me with a bite of chocolate cake in his mouth and a fleck of chocolate on the corner of his lip. "Um." He swallowed audibly and I burst out laughing.

"I'm just kidding," I said. I knew damn well why they did.

We both dug into our desserts and when we finished, Maddox asked about Kyle's parents. "You told me about the accident, but not about his parents. Has anything else happened?"

I shrugged. "I haven't heard from any lawyers, so that's a good thing, right?"

He nodded. "I take it they blame you for Kyle's death?"

"Oh, yeah. For sure." I wiped my mouth on my napkin and put it on my plate. "His dad calls me often to tell me just how much they blame me."

Maddox looked outraged. "He can't do that. That's harassment."

I shook my head. "They lost their son. I can't change them. It ruined their life."

"Do you think they'll really sue you for custody?" he asked.

I wished I knew the answer. "I have no idea."

"Well," he said. "I'm not a lawyer yet, obviously, but I've done some studying independently. Make sure you document any other encounters with them. If they call, write down what they say, the date and time, and so forth. Make a running log of anything, even if it seems insignificant."

"Thank you." I appreciated the advice. "I guess I need to consult a lawyer, just in case. Be prepared."

He pulled out his phone and tapped at it, and in a few seconds, mine dinged in my little handbag. "I sent you the names of the two lawyers I'd use if it was me."

"Thank you," I whispered. "It's nice to have someone in my corner."

"No matter what happens between us, I'll be in your corner," Maddox said. "You can count on that."

The waiter brought our check, and Maddox didn't blink an eye when I slapped down a twenty to cover my portion. He put a fifty down and told the server to keep the change. My jaw dropped.

"What?" he asked. "I'm not trying to show off. We just made that guy's night on a fifty-dollar tab."

I grinned at him and once again tried not to shiver as we walked out. He had his hand on my back again, but this time it was near my shoulder blades.

On my bare freaking skin.

Damn it.

Maddox opened my car door, but I didn't get in yet. I turned toward him and smiled up. "I had a nice time," I said.

He nodded. "I did, too. Can we do it again?"

I should've said no. We couldn't take this anywhere. I wouldn't force Tiffany on him or put someone in her life that didn't want her. "Yes, I'd like that."

Okay, then my mouth decided to make another date.

Maddox leaned in and my stomach clenched in anticipation. He was about to kiss me. In the split second it took for his lips to touch mine, I wished it could've led to more. An image of us writhing around on my bed flashed through my mind, and I opened my mouth in surprise.

His lips pressed softly against mine. It took all my willpower not to press my body against his, but as badly as I wanted to, it was way too fast.

Instead, I let my lips caress his ever so slightly, then pulled back. "Have a good night," I whispered, and slid into my driver's seat.

I glanced in the mirror as I drove away to find him standing exactly where I left him, staring at my car.

On the drive home, I found myself wishing he had said he wanted kids right away. We truly had gotten off on the wrong foot, and after our date, I wished it could be remedied. I could see myself growing quite fond of Maddox Kingston.

Chapter 10 - Maddox

The longer I stared at the laptop screen, the more confused I became. My official acceptance letter had come through. I'd opted for digital delivery, so when I logged in and found an email from the school in California, my stomach had churned.

But it wasn't excitement. Two or three weeks ago it would've been. But today, it was a mixture of dread and anticipation. I still yearned for freedom and space to be myself without my family breathing down my neck.

This week had taught me that Beth was a factor I couldn't ignore.

Not to mention my family. Did I really want to be so far away I couldn't drop in for dinner or a chat with my cousins or uncles? Or Mom and Dad?

What about Hailey? She'd turn into a woman while I was gone. Did I want to miss that?

Beth and I texted back and forth all week since our date. I didn't feel this much like a teenager with his first crush when I *was* a teenager with my first crush. She was funny and sweet and had a sarcastic edge that I loved, now that it wasn't directed with hostility toward me. I never imagined I'd get butterflies from talking to a girl, but there I was.

This was what I'd wanted to avoid. As exciting as the prospect of California was, and as sure as the counselor had been when she'd told me verbally that I should attend, I hadn't gotten an official acceptance yet. Now, it was right there in black and white.

I hit print and watched my small printer slowly spit out the paper. Then, I read it again. Nothing had changed. I was still accepted. I still had a big decision to make.

The best thing to do was to take it to my parents and lay it out. They were both smart. Dad got a taste of freedom when they moved. Granted, they just moved to Arizona, to my great-grandfather's territory, but still, it was a change. If anyone could understand, it would be Dad.

I still had my truck and wanted to put it back in the barn anyway. Stuffing the letter in my pocket, I grabbed my keys and wallet and headed out the door. When I pulled onto Main, I glanced over toward the grocery store parking lot to spot Beth pushing a shopping cart out of the store. I only got a glimpse of her, but it was enough to see she looked frazzled. I hadn't seen her since our date, so I turned around quickly in Stefan's garage parking lot and pulled in as Beth and Tiffany stopped the cart by her car. It was piled to the brim.

"Ma'am," I said through the open window in a deep and silly voice. "You look like you need a little assistance."

She laughed tiredly and looked at Tiffany, who whined.

"What's wrong?" I asked. She was normally cheery and vibrant.

"I'm not sure," Beth said. "She's been difficult all day. Maybe a growth spurt?" She shook her head.

Artemis growled when I studied her face and saw how exhausted she looked. "You take care of Tiffany, and I'll unload the groceries into your trunk."

She smiled in relief. "Thank you."

Bethany pulled Tiffany out of the small child basket at the front of the cart and cradled her in her arms. Tiffany whined and put her head against Beth's chest.

Her body temperature is high.

Just as Artemis tried to warn me, Bethany spoke. "She feels warm to me." She shifted Tiffany in her arms and cradled her head so she could press her lips to Tiffany's forehead. "Yes, she's definitely got a fever."

Tiffany let out a weird whine and burped. Immediately, Bethany reacted. "I know that sound." She yelped and flipped Tiffany, so she faced out away from her body, toward the empty part of the parking lot. As soon as she did, Tiffany projectile vomited.

Whoa. If she'd been facing me or her mom still, we would've been drenched. That was an insane amount of liquid.

I'd always prided myself on having a stomach of steel, but I had to clench my jaw as Bethany held Tiffany and pulled her hair back so it wouldn't get covered in vomit. I hovered uselessly and tried to think of what to do.

Inspiration struck, and I turned to the still-full shopping cart and yanked a bottle of water out of the package. When it seemed like Tiffany was done, I opened the bottle and handed it to Bethany. She helped Tiffany rinse her mouth out. "There's a blanket and a change of clothes in my trunk," she said. "Diaper bag."

I grabbed the pink and brown bag and rifled through it until I found a blanket and a baggie with frilly girly clothes in it, then held them out while Bethany helped Tiffany change. "I'll put the groceries in my truck and take them to your house if you want to take her to the clinic," I suggested.

Bethany looked at me with such a look of appreciation that I patted myself on the back for offering. "That would be amazing," she said. "I want to get her fever checked; she was fine in the store." She leaned into the car and buckled Tiffany in, then tucked the blanket all around her. "She was a little whiny, so I checked her forehead a couple of times and she was not feverish. It spiked fast."

"Go," I urged.

She handed me her house key. "If you park in the back, the stairs from the office go straight up into the kitchen." She looked at me with wide eyes, then threw her arms around me and squeezed me for a heart-stopping second. Without another word, she ran around her car and within seconds she backed away and drove out of the parking lot, leaving me and my truck and a cart full of food.

The urgent care clinic was on the outskirts of town, just in the county. Bethany's house was on the way, but by the time I loaded the truck up and returned the cart, she was long gone. I ran back toward the grocery store and grabbed their water hose on the side of the building, then hurried back to the dark spot on the pavement. I sprayed it until I saw no more chunks. It wouldn't have been fair to have left that for some unsuspecting cart-pusher to have to clean.

After putting up the hose, I drove to Beth's house. This time I parked all the way around back as she said. Using the key, I took a few bags and let myself into the silent downstairs. Walking into her home without her there felt like I was crossing a line of privacy, but I was still fascinated by it. Her office was one big room with two doors off of it. I looked around at the simple decor. Mostly there were pictures of Tiffany and who I assumed to be Bethany's parents. A man featured in many photos with Bethany. Probably Kyle.

Over the desk was a little wooden plaque thing that read "Mom--Boss--CEO." Cute. I didn't want to pry, but I had to find the stairs. The first door I opened was a simple bathroom. It was spotless. She was definitely a neater person than me.

The second door was the stairwell. Carpeted stairs muffled my footsteps. I opened the door at the top and stepped out into a bright, cheery kitchen. The island in the middle of the room was empty, so I put the bags there until I got them all in, then looked around.

Pale yellow walls made me think of Beth's happy personality, but the antique kitchen tools hanging up were a surprise. I stepped closer to look at the objects adorning the walls and recognized an old corn shucker, vegetable peeler, and biscuit cutter, among other things. Some were rusty, some looked new. None appeared to be used, just decor. It wasn't what I would've expected from Beth, but I liked it a lot.

A clock chimed somewhere deeper in the house, startling me.

Just get the groceries unloaded so we can go check on our girls.

Oh, they were our girls now? Plural? The idea of them both being mine somehow made me feel centered. Settled. I didn't take the time to study those emotions, just ran back downstairs and got as many bags as I could carry. It still took me two more trips to get it all.

The cold stuff was easy to put away. Freezer or fridge, not a lot of options. Going through Beth's cabinets to try to put the dry goods away was a step too far, so I organized them by type on the island and put all the grocery bags into a single bag. I'd noticed she used grocery bags in her bathroom garbage can downstairs, so I didn't trash them.

Once that was finished, staying at the house seemed again like going over my bounds, so I walked down the stairs, closing the doors behind me, then out to my truck. As I buckled my seatbelt, I heard the sound of a car on the road in front of Beth's house.

Sure enough, about a minute later, Bethany's car parked beside me. I jumped back out of the truck to help her, but there wasn't much for me to do. She pulled a sleeping Tiffany out of the back seat. "That was fast," I whispered.

"Miracle of miracles, there was nobody there when we went in." She grinned at me, and I rushed around her to open the door. "The pharmacy is delivering the medicine. It was totally worth the extra five bucks," she continued in a hushed tone as she walked through the office.

I went around her again and opened the door to the stairs. She smiled her thanks.

"What's wrong with her?" I couldn't get around her to open the top door, but I stayed close and when she got to it, I leaned in, pressing my front to her back.

Bethany's scent invaded my senses. I breathed deeply while I had the chance.

Unfortunately, my nostrils were super-strong, thanks to Artemis, and I also inhaled a nose-load of leftover vomit stink. Choking back a cough, I pushed the door open and Bethany walked through.

"Double ear infection," she said. "She got several her second year, and they talked about doing tubes, but then she stopped getting them. If the antibiotic shot doesn't work, we may decide to do it this year."

I furrowed my brow. "Tubes?"

She nodded her head toward the hallway. I inferred I would follow and stayed on her heels as she walked toward a bedroom. Through the open door, I saw a bed with a frilly pink and yellow bedspread. Tiffany's room. "Yeah, they put literal tubes through their eardrums to drain. Some kids are born with tiny inner ear canals and the fluid won't drain, then it gets infected. They say it's really not a big deal."

Once again, I darted forward and pulled down Tiffany's bedspread. Beth laid her down and took off her shoes and socks. "I knew as soon as she made that weird whine-burp what was happening. She *always* pukes when she has ear infections."

I watched in amazement as Bethany changed the sleeping child. She took off her shirt and walked out of the room. "Be right back," she whispered.

She returned a minute later with a wet washcloth. Tiffany slept like a rock through the washcloth all over her upper body, but especially her face and neck area. Bethany lovingly cleaned the still-flushed girl.

Her internal temperature has decreased just since she arrived here.

I couldn't tell Bethany that, of course. She still didn't know about Artemis and wouldn't for a long time. "She looks less flushed," I said instead.

"I think she feels cooler. They gave her oral medicine there to help the fever and ear pain. And the antibiotic shot should work pretty quickly, too." She pulled a nightgown with a unicorn on it over Tiffany's head, then I turned my head while she took off her shorts under the nightgown. At the least, it was the polite thing to do.

Bethany stood and backed away from the bed. I turned my gaze back to Tiffany. She looked like a little angel lying there. I couldn't believe how much affection I felt toward the little girl after we'd only spent a few minutes around each other. Bethany and I had texted back and forth so much I felt like I knew Tiffany better than I did.

"You're always showing up to help me," she murmured. Before I could reply, she pushed a button on a little device on the dresser, then walked out of Tiffany's bedroom.

"What was that?" I asked.

She chuckled. "You don't have much experience with kids?"

I shrugged. "My aunts and uncles are popping them out left and right but mostly I wait until they're old enough to play with before I give them much attention."

"It was a baby monitor." She walked down the hall and turned right into the living room instead of left into the kitchen. "So, I guess you're my new knight in shining armor?" She plopped down on the large, plush sofa and sighed.

The doorbell saved me from answering. I hadn't sat down yet, so I held up a hand when she started to get back up. "I got it."

It was just the prescription, so I signed for it and gave it to Beth.

She read the label. "She doesn't get any until morning since she got that shot in the office."

I looked around awkwardly. This room, besides lots of toys and a TV and entertainment center, had lots more pictures. "I looked at some of your pictures downstairs," I said.

"Mostly family." She watched me as I studied the photos in the room. It was more of the same people. Her parents, Tiffany, and Kyle. Oddly, I felt no jealousy or anger about all the photos of Tiffany's father. Probably because of all Bethany had told me about him, she never mentioned or acted like she'd been in love with him.

When I looked back at her on the couch, she looked lost.

She needs comfort.

I sat beside her and held out my arms. "You look like you need a hug."

Bethany signed and leaned over so I could wrap my arms around her. This time, I was able to inhale her scent without any gross interruptions. Artemis hummed his pleasure at having her so close.

I kept my arms around her until I felt the tension leave her body, then I gently slipped away. She looked nearly asleep. "Would it be okay if I stopped by tomorrow with lunch?"

"You don't have to do that." She rolled her head my way and smiled. "You're so much sweeter than I expected you to be."

My heart swelled in my chest and the need to take care of her grew stronger. "Don't say that. You'll ruin my reputation."

I pressed a kiss to her forehead and inhaled her scent one more time, then stood. "I hope your night is calm," I said and nodded toward the hall and Tiffany's room. "And that she sleeps like a baby."

Bethany stretched with her eyes screwed shut. Luckily. Otherwise, she would've seen my gaze fly to her chest as she stuck it out when she arched her back during the stretch. I walked toward the kitchen and the door to the downstairs office. "Have a good night," I called before I tried to do more than kiss her forehead.

Artemis wasn't helping. If he'd been in front of me, I was sure he would've been drooling, the perv. I told him to calm down as I jogged down the stairs, but he ignored me. Of course.

I left Bethany's and went straight to my parents' house. I needed my mom's help. As soon as I pulled in, Dad met me at the door. "You okay?" he asked.

"How'd you know?"

He shrugged. "A father can tell. I heard you pull up. You rarely come over without texting us first."

"I just need a recipe from Mom." I jogged up the porch steps. "Tiffany is sick."

A knowing look crossed his face. "Sure thing. She's in her office."

I walked through the house, the one my mother grew up in, and I'd come to think of as home. Was I able to move away from here? From my home? I'd only lived there for five years, but it felt like a lifetime.

"Mom?" I poked my head in her office door.

"Hey, sweetie. What are you doing here?" She walked around her desk and pulled me into a hug. "It's nice to see you."

"Thanks." I squeezed her tight. "I need a recipe for your chicken soup. The kind you always made us when we were sick."

She pulled back and looked at me in surprise. "Why do you need a chicken soup recipe?"

"Bethany's little girl is sick. Ear infection. It would be nice to be able to take them soup tomorrow for lunch, and I want to make it myself."

Mom's face softened and she grinned. "You got it."

I followed her to the kitchen where she took her wooden recipe box out of the cabinet. In the back was a small pencil and a few index cards. She fingered through the cards until she found the one that she wanted.

She talked about making the soup as she wrote, giving me instructions about how often to stir, when to add spices, and that I could cheat by buying a premade rotisserie chicken at the grocery store and cut a lot off of my cooking time. "You always wanted my soup when you were sick," she reminisced. "It was my Nana's recipe. I'm glad you want to

make it for Tiffany. It makes my mother's heart proud."
She flicked away an imaginary tear as I laughed at her.

Once she finished writing the recipe, she held it up but
didn't give it to me. "Are you sure about this? Once you
start down this path, there's no turning back."

I nodded. "I'm sure."

She handed me the recipe and stood. I gave her another
hug. "Thanks, Mom. I knew you'd help me."

We made plans to have dinner the next week, and I headed
toward my truck. Dad waited on the front porch.

"Once you fall in love with that little girl, there's no
escaping it," Dad said.

The acceptance letter still in my pocket got heavier. More
like having a brick in my pants instead of a piece of paper.

I considered how I reacted to Tiffany being sick, and I realized it was probably too late for me. My need to protect them was overcoming anything else. "See you later, Pop."

Dad saluted me. And that was that.

Chapter 11 - Bethany

I slept with the baby monitor next to my ear and woke up every time I heard the slightest sound, but Tiffany slept through the night. She didn't wake up until I sat sipping my second cup of coffee and scrolling through social media. "Mommy?" Her little voice sounded thin and reedy.

She shuffled into the kitchen. I held my arms open. "Come on, sweet cheeks."

My little monkey definitely still didn't feel good, because normally she would've bounded into my arms with a squeal. Instead, she walked slowly and held her arms up for me to lift her. "Poor Doodle," I crooned. "How are you feeling?"

"My head hurts and my neck hurts." She pointed to the front of her neck.

"You mean inside your neck?" Her pitiful little nod made me hug her close. She meant her throat. I wished desperately I could've felt the pain for her, but of course, that wasn't how life worked.

I lifted her in my arms and walked to the bathroom beside her bedroom. After rummaging around for a thermometer, I walked her through holding it under her tongue until it beeped. "Hey," I said and squeezed her tight. "Your fever is down. How about a popsicle to celebrate?"

She nodded almost eagerly. It was still very pitiful and lethargic compared to her normal levels of enthusiasm. I was just grateful her temperature was under a hundred.

"I'm sleepy," Tiffany whispered halfway through her popsicle. I figured she'd want to rest more. Ear infections always took it out of her.

We dropped the popsicle in the sink, and I hummed as I held my girl close, then tucked her into bed. After I got the correct dose of her antibiotic and gave her a bit of pain medicine, I stretched out beside her and thought about all the things her dad had missed over the three years since she'd been born. I liked to think he was there for it all, watching from heaven.

When her breathing was even and steady, I closed her bedroom door and headed to the kitchen. This was a good opportunity to get some cleaning in, starting with the groceries Maddox had laid out so carefully. He'd even put them in neat rows by food type.

By late morning, I'd made my way through most of the kitchen, disinfecting and wiping everything down, when my phone beeped on the island. It was a text from Maddox. **Hope you're getting hungry. On my way.**

He'd said he would bring lunch, but I'd been expecting him to put it off or something. I didn't know why I expected him to let me down but knowing for sure he was coming over set my stomach on fire. I had no idea what to expect.

The doorbell interrupted my vacuuming, and I nearly jumped when I heard it. Scrambling toward the door, I opened it to find Maddox on my doorstep with his arms full of paper bags. "Madd," I exclaimed. "You should've told me you intended to cook! I probably have some of the ingredients already."

He shook his head. "Nope, I didn't want you to have to worry about anything today. This is all on me." He leaned forward and pressed a firm kiss right on my lips. It took my breath away, to my chagrin. I didn't know why he affected me so strongly.

I mean, sure, he was super hot. But this was more a personality thing. When I was with him, the hotness factor melted away and he was just Maddox. I didn't sit and think about how hot he was.

"Ma'am, go back to what you were doing. I'll be in the kitchen." He nodded with his lips pursed and walked around me, through the living room, and into the kitchen. I loved my open floor plan, even more at the moment. It meant as he moved around the kitchen and I moved around my living room, I was able to watch him.

"May I have permission to find what I need?" he called over his shoulder once he'd unpacked his bags. I couldn't see all the ingredients, but he had a rotisserie chicken.

"You have permission!" I called.

He gave me a thumbs-up and shot a smile over his shoulder. I watched for a minute as he found a stockpot and poured a bunch of chicken broth into it. He glanced back once and caught me staring, so I went back to vacuuming, but my gaze kept slipping to the kitchen. Within a few minutes, he moved around like he'd been in my kitchen all his life.

By the time I had my living room dust-free, Maddox had cleaned the kitchen up and sat on the couch. "It'll be ready in about a half-hour. Just giving the vegetables time to soften and the flavors to mix well," he explained.

The house already smelled delicious. My stomach growled. I sat beside Maddox with the intent of kissing him—a real kiss. Slow, sensual.

But as soon as I leaned in, I heard Tiffany's bedroom door open. "Mommy?"

With a sigh, I leaned back and smiled at Maddox. "In here, sweet cheeks."

She walked in much brighter-eyed and with more energy than this morning. "I'm hungry."

Tiffany stopped dead when she saw Maddox.

"Hello," he said gently. "I'm Maddox. I'm friends with your mommy."

I'd never hand another man around Tiffany. Nobody but family and my girlfriends. This was entirely new ground for both of us.

She took it in her stride, jumping in my lap. "I'm Tiffany. I'm three." With her occasional lisp, it sounded like her th-words were f- words, but Maddox grinned at her.

They struck up a conversation about dinosaurs, and I sat back and watched with relief and deep happiness. For a man that didn't want kids, he sure had stepped up and taken care of Tiffany.

When his phone beeped, he jumped up. "Stay there," he commanded. Soon, he returned with steaming mugs of soup.

"My mom always put it in a mug so I could drink it. Then when your broth gets low, you eat all the yumminess at the bottom of the mug with the spoon and these crackers." He set a little tray in front of Tiffany, then handed me one. He sat close to help her. "Eat," he told me with a wink. "I'll make sure she doesn't spill."

I hadn't been able to eat a meal with Tiffany since she was an infant without having to jump and go back and forth making sure she was okay.

Looking a gift horse in the mouth wasn't my vibe, so I sat back and sipped the soup. It scalded my mouth, but flavors exploded on my tongue. "Madd," I exclaimed. "This is delicious!"

He grinned. "It's an old family recipe. My mom's and her nana's. As I said, she made this for me."

I blew on it to cool it faster so I could eat, and when the first mug full was gone, I hopped up for more. Maddox tried to take the mug and do it for me, but I held out my hand. "I can get my refill."

While I was in the kitchen, I filled up a mug for him and made his tray. "I'll take over Tiffany duty," I said and settled it in his lap. "Your turn."

Tiffany and Maddox laughed and talked while we all ate. It scared the bejeezus out of me. I didn't want Tiffany getting attached to Maddox. Why had I said he could come to bring lunch? That had been irresponsible of me, to say the least.

While Tiffany tried to spoon out the last bit of chicken from the bottom of her mug, Maddox put his hand on my leg. "Hey," he said softly. Tiffany didn't even notice him speaking. "We'll take it one day at a time, okay? This is new for both of us."

I nodded and calm washed over me. It would be okay. Maddox had a good heart, that much I was sure of.

After her soup, Tiffany asked to watch a movie. I started to turn it on in the living room, but she shook her head. "No. Mommy's bed."

I chuckled and relented. She was sick, after all. I didn't have a TV in her room. I was always afraid she'd wake up in the night and turn it on, then not sleep.

"Sure, come on." I left Maddox on the couch and carried Tiffany to the opposite side of the living room, where my master suite was. Pausing in the doorway, I turned back to Maddox. "I'm going to give her a quick bath. She feels clammy, probably from sweating through the fever."

He smiled and nodded. "Sure! I'll just finish up in the kitchen."

As I entered the bedroom, I couldn't help the huge smile on my face. He cooked and I didn't have to wash dishes? Hot damn.

By the time I gave Tiffany a quick bath, brushed her hair, found pajamas, and set her on the bed, it was nearly her bedtime. But I turned on the video anyway. She snuggled in and by the time I had her all tucked in, her eyes were already heavy. I knew she'd be asleep in minutes.

I had a king-sized bed, which I'd purchased when pregnant. I couldn't seem to get comfortable and I'd become convinced I needed an enormous bed.

It hadn't helped. Nothing had helped until I had Tiffany.

I tiptoed out of the room and when I glanced back, she was blinking rapidly, a sure sign sleep was imminent. The movie's opening credits weren't even done.

When I walked into the living room and looked toward the kitchen, I found Maddox hanging up the hand towel. My kitchen looked as clean as it had before he arrived. Which was pretty damn spotless, since I'd spent half the morning on it.

"Want to watch a movie?" I offered. I didn't want to eat his food then send him on his merry way. That felt too rude.

His face broke into an ear-to-ear grin. "Sure."

We settled on the couch. "How are you feeling?" he asked.

I sighed and leaned my shoulder against his. "I have to admit. This day was a lot easier with you here. Normally, that dinner would've been much more difficult, and I probably just wouldn't have eaten." I looked over at him and smiled, then leaned closer. When he pressed his lips to mine, I couldn't keep my nipples from pebbling against his arm. The way we'd shifted pressed me against him.

A low growl from Maddox set my body totally on fire. I hadn't been kissed this way in a very long time and my body reacted. I couldn't hide my whimpers when my hands slid across my waist.

If he stopped now, I was pretty sure I'd bawl my eyes out. "No," I whispered. "Please don't stop."

"Oh, I don't plan to," he murmured against my lips. "I think this evening should be all about you. What do you think?"

I was almost powerless to answer, but I forced my head to bob up and down, and he chuckled.

"I can't kiss you if your head is moving."

I gasped as he cradled my head between his palms, taking control of me, positioning me in just the way he wanted. His thumbs smoothed across my cheeks and his tongue flickered against my lips.

Yes. I wanted this. He always seemed to know exactly what I wanted. No. What I *needed*. From helping me with groceries to this.

He shifted, pressing me into the couch and lying across me as his tongue plundered my mouth and a growing bulge in his pants signaled his arousal.

He sucked in another breath, and I rubbed against him, searching for something. A release. More of him.

His answering groan sent a shower of sparks through my body. I pressed against him again and sighed before sucking in a breath as his tongue slid against mine.

He drew back. "You sound so good," he murmured before he nuzzled my neck, trailing kisses of fire across my skin.

I pushed my hands into his hair, anchoring my fingertips at his scalp, holding him against me, hoping he would never pull away. Well, maybe a little. A bit of movement would be pleasurable, for sure.

He chuckled when I pressed against him again. "There's no hurry. I've got all night for you."

I shivered at the promise in his tone.

He kissed lower, his tongue trailing over my skin as he unfastened my shirt. I arched against him, giving him better access to whatever he wanted to touch. Heat thrummed through my body, scorching me everywhere he lingered.

My nipples peaked, and he brushed the pad of his thumb over my bra. Thank God I had decent underwear on. Something small, black, and lacey rather than something big, beige, and decidedly granny.

I reached a hand behind me to unhook my bra, but he shook his head.

"Leave it on. I like the view."

I relaxed, and he moved lower still until he nudged his chin and mouth against the waistband of my jeans. My breath caught in my throat as I waited. Then I pushed gently against his head, urging him lower.

He lifted his head, and I glanced down my body, meeting his gaze. "You are Miss Hurry tonight."

"I know what I want." I grinned at him.

"Oh, yeah?" He trailed his hand between my legs, pushing the thick seam of my jeans against my aching clit.

I moaned, a needy sound I'd never made before with anyone else, not that there'd been that many. "Don't tease me."

"Hm?" He sounded completely distracted, but he absolutely wasn't, because he pressed against me again. "You mean, nothing like this?"

"No."

He looked up; his movements sharp as he assessed me with eyes that almost seemed molten. "No?"

"I mean, yes." Hell, what did I mean? "I mean—"

"Tell me what you want," he crooned. "Tell me, Beth."

"Touch me." I blurted the words out. They weren't tentative, but they weren't quite an order. More a plea.

"Is that all?"

"Just touch me, dammit." I surprised myself with the unexpected command, and he barked out a laugh.

"Yes, ma'am." He unfastened my jeans, and I shimmied my hips, lifting my thighs off the couch as he pulled my pants down and discarded them on the floor in a crumple of denim.

He ran his finger lightly over my panties, taking the same path he had over the seam of my jeans. "Touch you like this?"

I wriggled, looking for more. "Please."

Maddox moaned in response to my desire. "This?" He did the same thing again, and I sighed, exasperation warring with desire.

"You want me to take them off?" It would've been easier if I could've vaporized them with my mind.

"Do you want to?" he countered before sliding his finger under the fabric and flicking it softly against me as I moaned and gripped the throw draped over the arm of the couch.

I moaned and nodded. "Off is good," I ground out as I tried to control my breathing.

He braced his arms, and I glanced at him. "But the old-fashioned way. No ripping my expensive panties."

He grinned, and I couldn't be sure if he was disappointed or amused. Then he bent down between my legs and slid my panties down so slowly that every movement of them over my skin sent another shower of sparks through me.

I let my head drop back as cool air kissed my skin, then his tongue flickered across me, and I jerked like I'd been electrocuted. He did it again and again then nudged a fingertip just inside me as he sucked gently on me, rolling my clit beneath his tongue.

"Holy Mother of God," I squeaked out, and his answering chuckle sent vibrations of pure lust rocketing to my core.

He moaned like I was a five-star meal, and I tightened my thighs around his head, trying to keep him in place.

My hand found my nipple almost of its own accord, and I arched against him as two of his fingers moved inside me, caressing places I'd begun to think were mythical after so long giving myself orgasms.

My thoughts deserted me as he licked more and more. The dancing sparks meant I was only aware of him. I could only feel *him*. Maddox's name echoed through my mind, and I tasted it on my lips and my tongue as it emerged on a sigh. Somehow, I also heard something like a growl, but I was so unfocused I didn't register it as more than Maddox enjoying himself.

Hearing his name seemed to spur him on and every muscle in my body began to tighten, curling in on itself as I caught my breath, so I had nothing else to focus on but the way Maddox made my body respond to him.

My breathing became more rapid, and I closed my eyes to block out the senses. My thoughts swam, fracturing as I lost myself in the pulsing and fluttering of my muscles.

I'd never come so hard. "Did I…did I *pass out?*" I murmured, and Maddox laughed.

"Not unless you moan like that while you're unconscious."

My entire body was useless, just melted on the couch. "I feel like wet noodles or soggy bread."

He laughed again, the sound deep, and rich and mellow, and it gave me goosebumps. "I can honestly say no one has ever said that to me before."

"I've never felt like this before." Even my voice was slurred and drowsy. "Your turn?" Hope beat a quick tattoo in my heart.

I wanted to touch him, to please him the way he'd just pleased me.

"No." He held his hands out like he was warding me off. Then he softened his tone. "I mean, this was about you."

But my gaze zeroed in on the bulge in his pants. "You sure?"

"I am *so* ready." He stretched back out beside me. "Literally one touch and I'll go." He smiled, but desire lurked in his eyes as he stretched out alongside me.

"Oh, yeah?" Curiosity colored my tone.

"Yeah."

"One touch, right?"

He lifted one shoulder in a half shrug. "Something like that." But his voice deepened as I smoothed my hand down the front of his shirt, over his abs and cupped his cock.

"Just one touch," I whispered, and he pressed an open-mouthed kiss to my neck.

"I want so much more," he mumbled. "Just not tonight. Tonight was about you."

Disappointment flickered inside me, but I nodded. "Quick and dirty, then."

He thrust his hips against me. I took that as agreement and popped his button fly open before he could say anything else.

Maddox's cock was hot and heavy in my hand, and the skin slid smooth and soft as I stroked my fingers gently up the shaft.

He trembled. "Oh, shit. So close already." He gritted his teeth and pushed his hips forward again as I let him fuck my hand at whatever speed he wanted.

I pressed my other hand to the back of his head and guided him closer for a kiss, and his tongue thrust in time with his hips as I sucked gently on it.

He drew in long breaths through his nose and his movements became more urgent until he ripped away from me. His entire chest rumbled with a growl as hot cum spurted over my palm and fingers.

"Shit. Shit. Sorry. Fuck. Sorry about that." He sat up quickly and reached for my Kleenex. "That went so fast."

I tilted my head and looked at him. "Why are you sorry?" He seemed so embarrassed.

His cheeks colored a little. "For the mess?"

I laughed and shook my head. "No, Maddox. You should be sorry for depriving me of that cock moving inside me."

He grinned and looked down before meeting my gaze again. "Next time, I promise."

Chapter 12 - Maddox

As I squirted shampoo into my palm, the hairs standing up on back of my neck alerted me to their arrival. Artemis recognized family. I didn't get freaked out. It was either my uncles or my cousins. Or both.

They loved to show up unannounced and without invitation. Yet another reason the school in California had seemed so attractive.

Not that I minded my family being around. But maybe I didn't feel like having company today. Maybe I was in the middle of a marathon lovemaking session on my living room floor and they let themselves in. They could've gotten one hell of an eyeful.

When I walked out of the bathroom, sure enough, I spotted Rico and Jury through the bedroom doorway, sacked out on my couch with my PlayStation controllers in their hands. "Come on in," I called.

"Yeah, thanks." Jury's voice was full of laughter. "We appreciate the invite."

"Not that I'm not thrilled to have you both over, what are you doing here?" I yanked on underwear and toweled my hair as I waited on their reply. There was no point in shutting my bedroom door. If they wanted to talk to me, they would've just come on in anyway.

"We want to know what's going on with you," Rico replied.

"Yeah." Jury cursed. "Dammit, Rico." The chiming sound my TV made when it was turned off told me Rico beat Jury and it pissed him off. Typical Jury. "We've barely heard from you for over a week."

I opened my closet and took out a pair of my uniform pants. "I've been busy."

"Not working. I checked your schedule. What've you been doing?"

The activities of the night before flashed through my mind. Artemis hummed.

"Just hanging out." I tried to evade their questions.

Rico joined Jury in my doorway as I put on an undershirt and tucked it into my pants. "Do you two have to be here?" I asked with a sigh. "Is it totally necessary?"

"Yes." Jury raised his eyebrows. "So, Bethany?"

I hung my head. "What about her?"

"Have you finally admitted that she's your mate?" Jury walked into the room and launched onto my bed, tucking his hands behind his head as he bounced. "Or are you still trying to deny Artemis?"

"I admit she's my mate," I said reluctantly.

"Ha!" Rico crowed. "I told you."

Jury shook his head. "I figured he'd hold out a while longer."

"Are you two in high school?" I asked. This was what I hated most. I hadn't made up my mind yet. If I didn't know how I felt about Bethany, how was I supposed to explain it to them? "You gossip more than all the women in the family put together."

"More than Hailey?" Jury covered his face with my pillow. "That's harsh." His muffled voice was light and teasing, however. He wasn't mad.

Neither was I, not really. More aggravated at the complete lack of privacy. If it wasn't for Bethany—and now, also

Tiffany—I would've already accepted the California law school.

Not to mention, I'd never been one to kiss and tell. Jury and I had our fun with the girls in town and even a few towns over, but I didn't like to compare stories like they were some sort of conquest or something.

"Look." I faced them and buttoned up my uniform shirt. "I like Bethany. I like her daughter. That's all there is to say right now. We're taking things one day at a time. *Slowly.*"

Jury peeked out from under the pillow and his face was far too smug. "See? Things can happen super-fast. It wasn't long ago you two hated each other, right? Just like a week ago?"

Told you.

Artemis and Jury were both far too self-satisfied about the whole situation. "You can both shove it."

Rico held up his hands. "Hey!" he exclaimed. "I'm concerned for you, cousin, but why the attitude?"

"Not you," I grumbled. "Jury and Artemis."

When they realized I meant Jury and my dragon, they both burst out laughing.

"When are you going to tell her?" Rico asked when they stopped laughing.

I paused in the middle of buckling my belt. "Fuck," I whispered. "I hadn't thought about it."

"How could you forget about something that important?" Rico and Jury exchanged a look. "That's kinda big."

"I don't know. When I'm around her, everything feels so natural. It just slipped my mind." I sat on the bed and put on my socks, but my body reverberated with shock. How would I tell her? It could ruin everything. I'd heard stories of mates being torn apart because the female couldn't handle the news.

The whole situation made me melancholy.

Are you ashamed of me?

I'd never felt anything but uplifting emotions from Artemis. Sure, he got angry sometimes, but usually only if I was already angry. And he occasionally was irritated, usually at me for being a bonehead. But sadness wasn't anything he'd ever expressed before.

A wave of mourning washed over me, but the emotions weren't of my making. Artemis was sad that he thought I wanted to hide him.

"Just because I hadn't thought about it doesn't mean I'm not going to tell her," I told both Artemis and my cousins. "It won't be easy though. I'm a little worried she won't understand."

I wouldn't have chosen her if I didn't think she would understand.

Artemis was right.

"She'll understand," Rico said. "The cases of the humans rejecting the dragon shifters? All those old lores? When have you heard of it happening in the last several hundred years? All the stories are old. I think they're made up to make sure if a dragon finds his mate, he proceeds with caution to minimize complications."

He was probably right. "I haven't ever known it to happen," I admitted. "But I'd rather it not go bad before it gets better, either."

Rico and Jury nodded their agreements.

"This older woman has been hitting on me and it's kind of freaking me out," Rico said.

Before I could ask him who she was, my phone beeped my final warning. I liked to set reminders, so I got out the door on time. Otherwise, I always ended up procrastinating and got to my destination late. "We can catch up on you two later, okay?" I asked. "I gotta get to work." They hauled their asses off my bed as I put my gun, pepper spray, and handcuffs on my belt.

"Okay, but we're going out. This weekend." Jury pointed at me until I nodded.

"Okay, fine. You got it."

Once they had my assurance, they finally left. I grabbed my wallet, phone, and keys, and followed them out a few minutes later.

Since I lived so close, I liked to walk to work. My truck was back at the manor house in the barn, anyway, where I preferred to keep it. If I needed it fast, it was an easy walk to a path that led up through the woods to the manor. It would take a normal human a good half hour or more to walk it, but it only took me minutes if I let Artemis help me a bit.

All week, every shift, I gave myself plenty of time and walked slowly to work. That way I could call Bethany and see how her day was going. Today was no different, and why I'd been so insistent on getting out the door on time.

She picked up on the second ring. "Hey, Maddox." Her smooth voice warmed me and lifted my spirits.

"Hey, you." I tucked the hand not holding my phone into my pocket. "How are you? How's Tiffany feeling?" It had been several days since her dose of antibiotics, and my quick internet search had told me it should've at least begun to help.

"Like a new kid," Beth said happily. "She's totally back to normal. Of course, we have to give her the full run of antibiotics, so the ear infection doesn't take hold again, but she's wonderful."

Knowing Tiffany felt better made me happier than I'd expected it to. "I'm so glad to hear that. I've been thinking about you both."

She giggled and the sound made me want to compose poetry. What the hell? I'd never been sentimental like that before. "You just saw us yesterday."

I scuffed my toe on the sidewalk as I worked my way slowly toward the station. "I know, but it was nice seeing you. You've been on my mind."

"Well, about that." Some static came over the line and Beth's voice muffled. "Sure, honey. Get a yogurt cup. Yes, I bought the ones with the princesses on them." The phone rustled again. "Sorry, I'm back. What I was going to say was that my mom asked if Tiffany can spend the night tomorrow night. As long as she still feels good, I'm happy to let her go."

"Okay," I said. I thought I knew what she was getting at, but I needed her to spell it out for me. "That sounds nice."

"Yes, so if Tiffany isn't here, would you like to maybe come to stay the night? Here?" She paused while I contained my excitement and tried not to jump for joy in the middle of Main Street. "With me?"

"Sure," I said, barely containing the joy in my voice. "I'd love to." The thought of touching her again, her bare skin... Making her moan and orgasm. "I'll be there after my shift." The crack in my voice was purely coincidental. Not desire or anything at all. Nope.

"Perfect," she whispered. "I'll talk to you later."

I said goodbye with a lump in my throat. Suddenly, the day was brighter. Cheerier.

Seconds after hanging up, my phone beeped the sound for a new email. I rarely got emails, since I opted out of everything imaginable. I glanced at the notification and the beautiful day got darker when I saw who it was.

The law school in California. I opened it and read a canned form type letter about scheduling a tour of the campus and links for articles that were supposed to help a person choose a school. One of them was what to pack for dorm life.

The email reminded me that there was a huge rock in my gut that I had to figure out. School here in Colorado, one county over? Or California, where I'd finally get a taste of real freedom?

But I'd be leaving Bethany behind to do so.

It was my turn for patrol, and I carefully avoided Bethany's street. The words in the email form letter churned in my mind over and over.

I had the later shift, so I didn't want to call Bethany when I got off. I sent a text instead. **Hope you had a good day. Looking forward to tomorrow.**

She didn't respond, so I tossed and turned, going back and forth about the school, until finally, I fell into a restless sleep full of dreams I couldn't remember once I woke.

I had the early shift the next day, so I rushed around as soon as the alarm went off and hurried to the station without calling Bethany. A few minutes into my shift—desk duty this time—my phone beeped with a message from Bethany. **Sorry, I was exhausted last night. I'm looking forward to it, too! See you tonight. XOXO**

Her message brightened my mood considerably, and as the day went on, I grew more excited. She surely meant that we'd take things further than we had the other night. She'd specifically asked me to spend the night. That didn't mean watch a movie and cuddle.

I cut out a little bit early and headed to the only barbershop in town to get a professional haircut and shave. Nothing made me feel more like a man than having a straight-razor shave. As soon as the barber was done, I went home and showered, fixed my newly cut hair, and gave myself a pep talk in the mirror.

"Just because she invited you over for the night doesn't mean you get to expect anything," I told my reflection. "Take it slow. Take your cues from her. It'll all work out. She's your mate."

Artemis growled his agreement. *Mate.*

Even though I'd had sex before, too many times to count, this time was the most special. The most significant. By the time I rang her doorbell and stood on her stoop with a single lily that I'd hastily plucked from my mom's garden before coming to Bethany's, my nerves were shot. What if I'd read it all wrong? What if she wasn't ready for this?

Everything fizzled to a stop the moment she opened the door. She wore nothing but thigh-high sheer black pantyhose, a black lace garter, and a red lace and silk teddy. "Hurry," she hissed. "I don't want my neighbors to see."

I rushed inside and she slammed the door. My gaze stayed glued to her body. "Holy shit, Bethany. You're gorgeous."

Artemis purred and growled in succession. *Mine. Mate.*

Bethany put her hands on my shoulders and stood on her tiptoes. "I'm glad you're here," she whispered in my ear.

My instincts took over as I claimed her mouth. The lily lay on the floor, forgotten, as I scooped her up into my arms and walked across the living room toward her bedroom door.

It was time to claim my mate, even if I couldn't fully. Even if she didn't it know yet, Bethany was mine.

Chapter 13 - Bethany

Excitement fizzed in my veins as Maddox strode through my apartment with me in his arms. I nestled against his chest, loving the safety and security I found there. His heart pounded under my ear, and a low rumble echoed briefly through him.

"You hungry?"

He shook his head. "Nope."

I giggled. "Well, your stomach is going crazy in here. All this grumbling and rumbling."

"My appetite today is only for one thing." Without pausing in his stride, he shifted my weight and pressed a kiss to my hair.

I shivered and melted closer to the heat of his body. "I like the sound of that."

He pushed through my bedroom door and stood for a moment as he looked around the room. Thankfully, I'd tidied the house, throwing errant pairs of panties in the hamper and straightening the covers on my bed. I was a neat and clean person by nature, so there hadn't been a lot to do, but at least there would be no surprises.

"Nice." He nodded his head as I smoothed my palm over where his T-shirt covered his left pec.

"The bed is *very* comfortable." My purr was only faux-seductive, and he knew it because he met my gaze with amused eyes.

"You mean you wouldn't prefer a rug burn?" His eyes danced with merriment.

I stuck my tongue out, and he leaned forward and kissed it.

"Put me down. I want you naked." I wriggled from his arms, gratified by the prominent bulge already in the front of his pants.

He gripped the hem of his T-shirt and whipped it over his chest before balling it up and tossing it to the floor behind him.

My mouth dried at the sight of his muscular chest and his chiseled abs, and I reached out to touch him.

He backed away quickly and wagged a playful finger at me as he shook his head. "No touching."

"Oh." I smirked at him. "Are we in that dangerous *just one touch* situation again?"

His eyes widened briefly, and he shook his head. "No. In fact, I plan on fucking you all night long."

My legs wobbled at the conviction with which he spoke.

"Sounds…painful." But my voice came out too thin to carry off the joke.

"Never painful," he promised. "But I hope you have a fondness for orgasms."

Heat licked through me, and I nodded as he stepped toward me to cup one of my breasts through my negligee. He strummed against the nipple with his thumb, and it formed a hard peak through the fabric of my teddy. My breathing became more ragged, but I tried to maintain his gaze as desire lurked in the shadows in his eyes.

His lips parted, and he slowly bent toward me, taking forever before his lips finally met mine. I stretched onto my tiptoes, one hand steadying myself on his shoulder as I deepened the kiss, taking the lead and sliding my tongue over his lips.

He opened his mouth and kissed me almost lazily like he had all the time in the world, and he wrapped his arm around my waist, pulling me closer to him as his hand slipped from my breast, and he crushed me against his chest instead.

"Can you feel how much I want you?"

I nodded at his urgent whisper as his cock nudged against me through his pants.

"I'm really wet," I confessed, and he groaned at my admission.

I rubbed my thighs together, seeking friction, and he dropped his hand to where my thighs met. Then he dipped his finger between them. "You certainly are," he confirmed.

When he claimed my mouth again, it was with more urgency, and I would have melted into a pool of desire on the floor if he hadn't been holding me up. I pressed my hands between us and worked the buttons on his jeans before pushing them roughly from his waist.

He'd promised me more this time, and I was damn sure going to make sure he delivered.

His hands roamed all over me—underneath the teddy, over it, setting every inch of me alight, and I smiled in satisfaction at the success of one small outfit change.

"I'll have to wear this more often if it gets this reaction from you," I said between pants as he kissed the side of my neck.

"Oh, yeah?" His words were a low growl.

"Yeah. I'm thinking while cleaning the house, running errands, going to the store." I paused and waited for his reaction, almost knowing it would be a territorial one.

I didn't have to wait long.

"Mine." The word was part growl, part roar as he lifted me off my feet and laid us both out on the bed in one fast movement. He stretched over me and pushed his jeans off the rest of the way.

Excitement blazed through every part of me at the lust and possessiveness in his eyes, and I basked in being the one to incite it.

"Mine," he said again, but more gently this time.

"What's yours?" I teased.

He tucked a lock of hair behind my ear and fluttered kisses over my face. "This," he murmured. More kisses tracked down my neck. "And this." He drew down my spaghetti straps and revealed the curve of each of my breasts before trailing his tongue along their curves. "Definitely these."

I shifted restlessly beneath him, desperate for his touch where I wanted it most. "Stop teasing me."

He drew away and looked at me, one eyebrow lifted in a way that made him look amused. "I'm just wondering how much more persuasion you needed not to wear this to the store."

"None." I pressed against him again. "None." I paused. "I'm yours." At that moment, I meant it fully. I'd worry about later, well, later.

Maddox's expression changed and lines of tension formed on his forehead. He closed his eyes as he held himself stiffly above me, opening a gap between us. He sucked his breath through his nose like he was fighting for control, but when he opened his eyes again, they showed no strain.

"I'm glad to hear it." He lowered back toward me, pressing against me with just enough weight as he nestled himself between my legs. He traced his hand down my side, and I tensed to withhold my shudder.

"Tickles," I ground out.

"Oh. Sorry about that." But he did it again anyway.

His progress to where I most wanted him was excruciatingly slow, and I widened my legs in a blatant invitation. Cool air teased across my skin, and my arousal spiked.

Maddox breathed in and the look of focused strain crossed his face again.

"You okay?" I whispered the words because I needed him to be okay and finish this.

He nodded. "You just smell amazing."

Before I could respond, he pressed a finger against my clit, and I gasped at the sudden stimulation. He rolled it gently, and I moved my hips towards him, gentle thrusts that I couldn't have controlled if I wanted to. I lifted my head and kissed his neck, sucking the skin into my mouth.

He growled. "Yes, mark me."

I gasped out a giggle because it had been a long time since my hickey days, but another low growl rumbled through his chest.

He dipped a finger into me, and his cock lay hot and hard between our bodies. I slid my hand down and touched the tip of it, and a tremor ran through him. I smoothed the bead of precum over the head, and his breathing increased.

"I'm not coming against your belly like a teenager." The strain in Maddox's voice had grown tighter.

"Well, good. You promised me more this time." I grinned as I stepped up my stroking, contorting my body to reach the base of his cock before drawing my hand up the shaft.

He shuddered and gasped above me. "Do it again."

I did, and he groaned as he thrust gently against the movement of my hand.

"You're perfect," he whispered.

"I want to taste you." The idea sprang into my mind and the words came straight out of my mouth.

"Fuck. You got so wet when you said that." He groaned again and seemed to gather his composure before rolling us both over, the movement smooth, so I ended up straddling him.

I looked down at the way his cock rested against his abs. "I like this view," I murmured, and I teased the underside of his shaft with my fingers.

He shifted beneath me, and I grinned at the power I held over him. Then he reached up and pressed his palms to my breasts, using his thumbs to tease both nipples.

I shifted my position, dropping down into the space created by his spread legs, and I bent over his cock, blowing a soft breath over it.

"Fuck," he ground out. "Stop teasing me, woman."

I trailed my fingertip up and down him again. "Turn-about is fair play," I murmured, but really, I was just buying time.

His cock was huge. Bigger than I'd really accounted for, and I leaned forward, allowing my hair to brush the tops of his thighs. I grinned as the muscles there tensed.

A pep talk ran through my head. It wasn't my first time at oral. I could stretch my lips around that. Hell, I *wanted* it in my mouth, and what I wanted, I could achieve.

I licked slowly up the shaft, and he groaned. His hands were suddenly in my hair, fisting two big clumps like he was trying to anchor himself. When I reached the tip, I sucked it into my mouth quickly and briefly, releasing it, and Maddox let out a shuddered breath.

I took him into my mouth again, widening my lips around him, and bobbing my head down to take another inch inside. He groaned but stayed perfectly still, allowing me space and time to become comfortable with his size.

As I lowered my head further, allowing him to fill my mouth, I cupped his balls, gently rolling them between my fingers, and stroked his shaft where I hadn't reached it with my tongue yet.

Just when I was at the point of having to choose between more cock or air, he tugged at my hair, lifting me away.

"I don't want to come down your throat, either, Beth."

I lifted an eyebrow.

"You have no idea the things you do to me." His words were a low rumble, and he brushed my hair back from my face again, securing it behind my ear. "I want to be inside you."

I heated at his words, anticipation making me wetter and more desperate. Maddox suddenly growled, securing me against him and rolling us over again as his cock nudged against my entrance. I parted my legs and tilted my hips toward him as urgency rode through me in a wave.

He chuckled at my silent insistence but gave me what I wanted most, and I let loose a soft sigh as he pushed gently inside, stretching me to my limits. I drew back before pushing forward again, the concentration on his face showing the control he was exerting.

"You can go faster." The stretch felt amazing.

"I don't want to hurt you." Sweat glistened on his brow. "Ever."

"I'm not so fragile." Then I grinned at him as I thrust upwards, surging toward him and taking all of him in at once. I caught my breath, but the sudden sting subsided quickly as my body lubricated us. "See?"

He groaned. "Fucking hell. I didn't know it could feel like this." He waited another second. "It's never felt like this before."

Damn. That was one hell of a compliment.

His movements were slow at first, almost tentative, but I wrapped my arms around him and pushed my fingertips into his ass cheeks, then around his back as I draped my legs over his hips, allowing him deeper access.

He pressed against all the right places, and his breaths filled my ears as I searched for skin I could reach to kiss. Taken by a sudden urge, I pressed my teeth against his shoulder and bit down softly, although not hard enough to break the skin.

His entire body went rigid above me. "Christ." He sucked in an inhale as if something had startled him. "I'm going to come. I need you to come, too, Beth." He thrust into me, skin slapping against skin, his cock stroking all the right places, and my excitement built until he was my every thought, smell, taste.

I tensed around him, and he roared a final push as I pulsed, my body squeezing and relaxing around him.

"Holy shit." His chest rose and fell with big breaths. "That wasn't just sex." He settled some of his weight on me as he rested on his elbows. We both panted for a minute, foreheads pressed together as we rode the aftershocks of the best orgasm I'd ever had.

A smile slipped across my lips. "That was *very good* sex," I agreed, and I pulled him down for a kiss.

The rest of the night was filled with eating, feeding each other, and falling back into bed. We'd both been in such a hurry that the thoughts of condoms hadn't occurred to either of us.

Completely irresponsible on my part. But I was on birth control. It helped with my periods and ensured if I ever did manage to find myself a suitable one-night stand, I was covered.

Maddox assured me he was clean and that he didn't really live up to his playboy reputation.

I believed him.

The next day, it had taken us several false starts and several more orgasms to get out of bed, but eventually we managed it, parting ways after a late breakfast. He had a shift and I had to go get Tiffany. That didn't stop us from texting each other repeatedly throughout the day with increasingly flirty innuendo.

Monday dawned bright and cheery, and I couldn't help the smile still plastered on my face. Maddox had to work this morning, but he'd texted me on his walk to the station. I was already up getting Tiffany ready. We had to come to look at a new property and this one wasn't in too bad of shape, so I didn't mind bringing her. She loved to ride along with me.

My phone began to ring as I stepped out of the car, so I opened the back door so Tiff could get out and explore and answered the call. It wasn't a number I recognized, but that happened a lot in my business. Renters called from unknown numbers, property managers or realtors called to see if I had any interest in buying their properties, and so on.

"Hello, this is Bethany Leeds."

"Ms. Leeds. My name is Martha Brennen I've been retained as counsel for the Bearth family." My stomach dropped to the ground. They'd actually done it. They hired a lawyer. Those complete and total assholes. I opened my mouth to tell her to shove it, but she beat me and spoke before I could. "I apologize for calling you out of the blue, but since you have no lawyer for me to go through, I had no other option."

"What do you want?" I asked through clenched teeth.

"The Bearths have officially filed for custody. I'd like to set up a mediation so we can all sit down and try to come to some sort of agreement to keep this mess out of court."

My blood boiled with anger and outrage. "How dare they?" I seethed. "I am a good mother. I will not go to mediation. You can just sue me for custody. See you in court."

I hit the button on my cell to hang up on her and wished for the old days with clunky house phones. They'd been so satisfying to hang up on someone with.

My anger boiled as Tiffany ran around the yard with a stick, completely oblivious to the phone call I'd just had, thankfully. At least this hadn't affected her. The one meeting we'd had with Kyle's parents, in the park, had been just a blip on her radar. She'd forgotten it almost as soon as it happened. Almost falling off the monkey bars had been a more lasting memory.

I found the key and walked the house, and tried to make notes that Kara would want, but I had to look at the same things over and over because I couldn't focus. Tiffany ran from room to room once I gave the home a look-around to make sure there weren't any missing pieces of floor or random nails. Once, in a property I hadn't bought, I'd even found evidence of squatters, complete with old needles. Since then, I at least looked around first, and always had my pepper spray in my pocket.

After several minutes of trying to focus and failing, I gave up. "Come on, Tiff," I called. "We'll come back. Mommy needs to call a friend."

"Who? Can I come?" She came careening out of the back bedroom and stopped in front of me. "What friend, Mommy?"

"I'm going to call my friend Maddox. He can give me some good advice. Let's get you home first, okay?"

She nodded. "Maddox was nice, and he makes yummy soup."

Since she didn't ordinarily like soup, the fact that she'd eaten Maddox's so well had been a miracle. I hoped it meant some of her picky eating habits were going to fade soon. The parenting books said picky eaters often got more adventurous as they got older. I sincerely hoped that was true.

After helping her buckle into her high-back booster, I headed back toward our house. Along the way, I changed my mind and decided I'd much rather talk to him in person. He'd told me he was on desk duty and would be at the station all day. "Tiff," I called over my shoulder. "Do you want to go see a real police station?"

She squealed in excitement, as I'd hoped she would. "Yes!"

We drove past our road and on toward town. I couldn't tell if Maddox was inside since he rarely drove, so I texted him. **Hey, are you at the station?**

His reply was only seconds later. **Yep.** Followed by, **Bored to death. Mondays are the worst.**

Well, good then. I got Tiff and hurried inside, anger still coursing through me. The thought of Kyle's parents somehow possibly succeeding and taking my sweet girl away from me made me a mixture of panicked and terrified.

And beyond furious.

Maddox jumped up in surprise when we opened the door and stepped in. I'd never actually been inside. It was like I would've imagined a small-town sheriff's office would look. A couple of rows of desks, with just a couple of doors leading off the main area. There was a reception area with a small wooden waist-high fence that blocked the office area of the station from the waiting area.

"Hey," he called. "I didn't imagine you'd be here after that text." He shook his head. "Surprised I didn't know," he muttered.

"How could you have known?" I walked through the small swinging door toward him.

Tiffany bounded through then ran around me. "Hey, Maddox! Mommy took me to an old yucky house, and I saw three spiders and there was dirt everywhere."

He squatted beside her and wiped a smudge of dirt off of her cheek. "I see that. Was it haunted?" Maybe I wasn't as good of a mother as I thought I was. I hadn't even noticed the dirt on her face in my preoccupation.

She threw her hands in the air and started making ghost sounds and twirling in circles. Maddox returned his attention to me. "What is it?" he asked.

I glanced at Tiff. "I got a phone call." I spoke as quietly as I could while she ran around the desks making ooooh noises.

Maddox picked up on my reluctance to talk around Tiff. "Hey, Tiffany, do you want to see the jail cells?" he asked.

She squealed in excitement and jumped up and down. "I just cleaned them," he whispered to me. "No prisoners here, and I'll unlock the locks so she can explore."

I nodded. He walked to one of the doors leading off the office area. I followed into a room with two cells and old-fashioned iron bars. Tiffany loved watching an old TV show about a country police officer and his bumbling deputy with her grandfather. This looked so much like that show that she recognized it immediately.

He opened the doors. "Here," he said. He propped the doors open with a couple of chairs. "Now she can't even pinch her fingers if she tries to close them."

"Is this where you keep the bad guys?" she asked with wide eyes.

"You got it. They stay here until it's time for them to go to a bigger jail or if they're not really all that bad, they get to go home."

Tiffany nodded somberly. "Wow."

"Go see," he said, and waved her toward the two cells.

She skipped forward and the first thing she did was push the button on the toilet to flush it in the first cell. "You cleaned those well, right?" I asked with a curled nose.

He chuckled. "With bleach. The worst thing that'll happen is they might not be totally dry, and she'll get bleach on her clothes."

I could've lived with that. While Tiffany spun circles inside the cell with her arms out, I told Maddox about the phone call.

Maddox's arm went around me from behind as soon as I started talking. A bit of comfort, and I was glad to have it.

"Don't worry. I'm not a lawyer yet, but I've been researching it, just in case. They don't have a case."

Tiffany ran from one cell to the other and ignored our talking completely.

"Just in case they do, we can call one of the names I gave you, okay?" He squeezed my side.

I gladly leaned my head on his shoulder. "Thank you," I whispered.

"In the meantime, let me have the number of the gal that called. She absolutely shouldn't have contacted you that way. She was supposed to send you a letter, preferably certified."

I nodded and pulled it up on my phone with my head still on Maddox's shoulder. If Tiffany noticed her Mommy being held by a man that was supposed to just be a friend, she didn't seem to care.

"We'll go to the lawyer's office together. I'm by your side on this, okay? All the way."

I handed him my phone and wrapped both arms around his waist. How had I gone so quickly from not liking him very much to being so relieved to have him here with me? I wasn't sure when that had happened, but however and whenever it did, having someone on my side fully was an enormous comfort.

"Everything is going to be okay," Maddox said. "I promise."

For whatever reason, the tension inside me melted nearly away. And I fully believed him.

Chapter 14 - Maddox

Flying with Artemis was always some of the most centered and focused times for me. Things seemed to fall away, and worries disappeared. We focused on the air and the smells of the forest, of going as high as we could, then diving down until the treetops brushed his belly. Everything was about adrenaline and ecstasy.

But not today. Today, I kept thinking about California and Bethany. I knew she'd get through the custody battle without losing Tiffany. There was no doubt in my mind, so though that was going to be a headache and definitely would be stressful for Bethany, I wasn't worried. We already had a good lawyer who had agreed to take the case. Sometimes having the last name of Kingston was a real boon. As soon as I'd called, he agreed. That was fine with me because he was the best.

What worried me was losing her once I told her I was considering law school several states over. But while we were shifted, it was all too possible to project thoughts, which wasn't what I wanted to do, so I tried to think about other things and focus on the flight.

It wasn't as easy as I'd hoped. Artemis kept us in the air for a long time, though, and by the time we landed in the woods near the manor house, I did feel somewhat better. I'd been avoiding shifting and flying anywhere but our family land where we were extremely unlikely to find any humans wandering. Not only did we have no trespassing signs posted everywhere, but there was also something about the dragon and wolf territory that humans shied away from, especially human males. They would feel uneasy hiking in areas we frequented and would naturally find themselves heading away and back to their comfort zones. It was a rare thing for a human to stumble across dragon or wolf land, and here in Black Claw, we had both. Our agreement with Carlos and his wolf pack meant they roamed the land while we roamed the skies. It worked out very well for all involved.

I shifted back to my skin and walked out of the woods to find my grandfather leaning against the small outdoor shower he'd built just for us to use when shifting. We had a place for our clothes, showers, and everything we needed to clean up if we had a messy shift. Plus, it gave us some modesty.

"Son, you're projecting some pretty deep thoughts, you know," Grandpa said.

I nodded. "Let me get dressed."

"I'll be on the porch if you want to talk."

As I pulled my clothes back on, I considered how much I wanted to tell him. My upcoming choice weighed so heavily on my mind. It would've been nice to have someone to confide in, and I trusted my grandfather. He wouldn't reveal my secret or problems until I was ready for him to, that was for certain.

When I was dressed and had my boots back on, I joined Grandpa on the porch. He held out a glass of tea. "Okay, son. Want to unload on your old gramps?"

I chuckled and sipped the tea, which had a hint of oranges. Grandma's special recipe. "Thanks." I looked into his wise eyes and knew he'd help me figure out the best course, whatever that might've been. "You know I want to go to law school."

He beamed. "And I'm so proud that you do. You're going to be the best of us all, I can already tell."

I ducked my head. "Thanks. There's a problem, though."

Grandpa's brow furrowed. "What could it be? Your grades were exemplary. I thought you were already accepted to the school. Money isn't a problem."

"That's just it. I was already accepted. To two schools."

Recognition flew across his face. "Ah. Where is the second school?"

"California," I muttered.

He winced. "We don't have any family in California."

"Please don't take this the wrong way, but that's part of the draw." I said it as gently as I could, but his eyebrows still flew up. "No, it's not bad. It's just... I've never been alone. I've never had to do anything on my own. I went from it being just me, Mom and Hailey to this huge family, which is great." I held up my hands because he still looked confused. "I love the family and wouldn't trade them for the world."

"But?"

"But it would be nice to have a little bit of independence. And maybe some privacy."

Grandpa chuckled. "I've had those feelings before. When I lived with my father in Arizona. That's why I moved to Black Claw, Maddox. And you're an alpha. You're going to have those emotions probably even stronger."

"You left home," I said. A weight lifted off my shoulders. He knew what I meant. He understood. It was such a relief just to share the things I'd been worried about with someone else.

"I did. And it was the right thing for me. Only time will tell if it's right for you. But, Maddox, wherever you go, you have to make sure you have a place to shift. You have to have privacy and cover."

I nodded. "I've considered that. And of course, it would be a huge factor in my decision. And the family. And now, Bethany."

"Whatever you decide, we will support you. All of us will. We can visit you, and of course you know you're always welcome here." He smiled at me and shook his head. "I hate how much time I missed out on with you. We won't miss any more, even if you're living far away. We'll figure it out. Maybe I'll even let you kids teach me how to do that video chat stuff."

It was my turn to shake my head. "That'll be the day."

"If it's your dream to go to law school in California, we'll find a way to make it happen. But if it's a need for privacy and independence, then we simply need to set some ground rules for the family. You could even find a place a bit farther away during school if you opt to go here in Colorado."

I nodded thoughtfully. "I'd considered that, too. Just telling everyone would feel like such a rejection. I haven't wanted to come out and say sorry, guys, you're too invasive for me."

Grandpa shrugged. "It's not a rejection. We're a pushy, meddlesome bunch." He leaned forward and whispered, "They get it from your grandmother."

I burst out laughing. "I won't tell her you said that, so you don't get into a bunch of trouble."

"Appreciate that, son." He sighed and leaned back. "You can't keep this to yourself. You need to confide in your parents. Your cousins. We can all help you figure out the best course and support you on your journey."

"I will," I promised. "Soon."

We sat and continued to talk about the schools. I even told him about Bethany's legal troubles with Tiffany. He was as sure as I was that they wouldn't amount to much.

As the morning wore into the afternoon, my stomach growled, and my phone beeped at the same time. I checked it to find a text from Bethany. **Picnic at the park with Tiffany, if you're free.**

"Gotta go," I told Grandpa and jumped up. "I'm going to meet Bethany in the park."

Grandpa chuckled. "Boy, you've got it bad."

I knew what he was thinking, even if he didn't project his thoughts. He thought I could never leave Bethany.

And he was probably right.

I used my preternatural speed to take me down the path from the manor to just beside town. The path came out by the drive-in where my Dad had nearly killed another dragon who came back later and tried to get revenge. He was dead now, of course. That tended to happen when someone messed with my family.

A few minutes later, I crossed the greenway and entered the park behind the town proper. Bethany already had a blanket spread out on the grass near the jungle gym.

"Hey," I called.

She turned and gave me one of her thousand-watt smiles. She had the ability to melt every worry away with just one look and make me feel like nothing mattered but her. And when it boiled down to it, nothing mattered more, not really.

Tiffany ran up chattering excitedly.

She matters.

Artemis rarely expressed affection about anyone. Except for Bethany, of course, he'd wanted to claim her from moment one. He had developed feelings of affection and protection toward Tiffany in the couple of weeks we'd been around them.

Interesting.

"Maddox," Tiffany squealed. She ran up to me and held her hands up. I swung her up in the air and let her fly a bit before catching her and holding her tight as she squealed. "Do it again!"

I complied, throwing her up a few more times before Bethany interfered. "Okay, that's enough. She already ate a sandwich and she'll be puking all over you if you keep that up."

I'd seen the girl puke once before. She was a pro at it, leaving me with zero desire to repeat the experience while I held her.

"Go play," I encouraged, then plopped down on the blanket beside Bethany.

"She really likes you," she said. "Whatever happens between us, I'll expect you to be cognizant of that. I know you don't want kids."

She handed me a sandwich. I took a bite without paying any attention to what it was. It could've been sand and dirt and I would've eaten it if Bethany gave it to me. "I am," I said. "And I do want kids. I just think having a baby right now would be complicated." I chewed and thought about it. "Although, to be perfectly honest, if I had a child, I'd be very lucky to get it away from my mom, aunts, and grandmother." I rolled my eyes. "Not to mention my sister."

Bethany giggled. "I'm sure Tiffany would love to meet your sister."

"You have a sister?" Tiffany plopped down on the blanket. I knew she was walking up but hadn't realized she was within earshot.

"I do," I said. "And she loves to babysit. Maybe we can all go do something fun one day soon."

The sweet girl grabbed an apple and handed it to me. I wasn't planning on eating an apple, but when a three-year-old hands me an apple, I eat the damn apple. "Here you go, Maddox."

The way she said my name was so cute. It was more like Maddos or maybe Maddoth. She had the slightest lisp. "Thanks! Apples are my favorite."

"Me too," she crowed. Soon we finished our apples and she'd told me every food she liked and had begun the foods she didn't like. I tried to agree or disagree as was appropriate, but mostly I marveled at how cute she was and how surprised I was that I was actually interested in the little girl's food preferences.

"Tiff," Bethany interrupted gently. "You better go get some slide time in before we have to go."

She jumped up and ran off, but before she got far, she whirled around and came back. "Will you slide with me?" Tiffany asked shyly.

Nothing in the world sounded like more fun at that moment. Not even sitting in the warm sun with Bethany. "I'd love to."

If nothing else, I had to give Tiffany the medal for being tireless. Even with my dragon endurance, I finally had to call uncle. "Okay, you got me beat," I said. "I can't take one more trip down the slide."

My butt was sore and my hips from being a little bit too big for the narrow opening. I kept getting stuck halfway down.

She giggled. "You're too big to slide."

She was not wrong. I hobbled over to Bethany and stretched out on the blanket. She'd cleaned away the food, leaving plenty of room. "You're sweet to humor her like that," she said.

After making sure Tiffany wasn't looking, she leaned in and pressed a soft kiss to my lips.

Artemis wanted to deepen it and wrap her up in our arms, but we were in the middle of the park with kids and parents everywhere. I was lucky I got the quick kiss I did.

When the day wore on and Tiffany began to get visibly tired, Bethany smiled at me. We'd been holding hands for the last hour or so as Tiffany ran around with a girl she knew from school.

"Come on, sweetheart," Bethany called. We'd spotted Tiffany rubbing her eyes. "It's time to go home!"

She ran over, definitely slower than she'd been a couple of hours before. "But Mommy!"

Bethany held up one hand. "We've been here most of the day. Don't argue, okay?"

Tiffany's shoulders slumped, but she didn't voice another protest. She just trudged toward us. To my surprise, she came straight to me and held her arms up. "Carry me?"

My heart prickled as I drew her up into my arms. She laid her head on my shoulder. "Thanks, Maddoth."

Bethany looked ready to cry, and I even found myself a little misty-eyed. Tiffany had wound herself tightly into my heartstrings.

I carried her to the car and buckled her in while Bethany put the picnic supplies on the other side. Then, I walked around and put my hand on Beth's shoulders. "That was a nice afternoon," I said.

Beth peered into the car. "She'll be asleep before we hit Main Street."

I chuckled and pulled her into a hug. "Text me tonight."

After another soft kiss, she got in the car, and I watched them drive away.

It was time for a conversation with my father. I followed the trail back to Main Street, across and past the drive-in, and up the path into the woods. I knew exactly where to cut across to come out near my parents' cabin instead of my grandparents' or my Uncle Axel's place.

My father, alpha of the territory, was on the porch waiting for me when I came out of the woods. Of course, he'd known I was coming. He was more intuitive than I was, even though Artemis and I were alphas as well. "What's wrong?" he asked.

"Nothing. I just wanted to get your perspective," I said. "About Hailey."

He furrowed his brow. "Is she okay? Is something wrong?"

Shit. I hadn't meant to make him think she was the focus of my worries. "No, no, she's fine. I'm more thinking about what it was like becoming her stepfather."

He nodded somberly. "I don't consider myself that. Hailey is mine, no matter who fathered her."

I long suspected he felt that way. She called him Dad, just like I did.

"But I won't lie. It was scary at first. Suddenly, I had two kids. As thrilled as I was to have you both, it was slightly terrifying. I didn't know anything about raising kids. I still feel like I don't half the time."

"Yeah, me too." How badly could I screw up a kid? Probably pretty badly.

"But it works out. You do your best and try to do right by everyone involved. You're a good kid, Maddox." He put his hand on my shoulder. "And you'd make a great father or stepfather. Trust yourself in that, but make sure before anyone's heart gets too involved that you're ready for it. I don't think anyone would fault you for waiting a little while before getting too serious."

She was my fated mate. I'd fault myself.

Chapter 15 - Bethany

The diner hummed with business that didn't slow down for a second, even in such a small town. I slid into the booth with Kara. Abby had already ordered our teas. She'd texted this morning and asked if we wanted to do lunch. Of course, I'd agreed. We hadn't had a chance to hang out since the night we'd sort of argued in the bar about how I was treating Maddox. That had been nearly two weeks ago now and a lot had happened since then.

Kara and I had gone back this morning and checked out the house I couldn't focus on when Kyle's parents called, and we'd decided it was a good investment. It was a friend of Kara's who was selling it, so she'd given me first dibs on it. We'd talked about the possibilities all the way to the diner, both of us growing excited about what the property would be once we had some time with it.

When we sat down, Kara told Abby about the house, but the tension between Abby and me was pretty thick. She'd been standoffish since the scene at the bar.

"I apologized," I blurted out when Kara ran out of things to tell Abby about the house. "To Maddox. And now we're..." I blushed and looked down at my tea. How could I describe what Maddox and I were now?

"You're what?" Abby's eyes widened and she smiled at me. "Are you talking?"

Kara snorted. "They're doin' it."

Abby squealed, but luckily for me, the noise of the diner drowned it out. "I'm sorry I got in the middle of it," Abby said. "I should've let you two work it out and minded my own business." She pursed her lips. "Jury kind of got onto me for butting in, and now he won't tell me anything about you two."

I held out my hand and she took it. "It's okay. I get really prickly when things don't go exactly my way. I didn't make any of this any easier."

Abby squeezed my hand. "So tell me! You're doing it?"

After pulling my hand back and covering my face, I peeked out at her. "I don't want to kiss and tell."

That told her all she needed to know, though. More squeals from both Abby and Kara, but these didn't go unnoticed in the busy diner. A few people nearest us gave us odd looks. I shushed my friends with tears of laughter in my eyes.

"We're getting to know each other. And the more I learn about him, the more I like."

"How is he with Tiffany?" Abby asked. Kara and I had already discussed it.

I sighed. "You know I've never had anyone around Tiffany. No guys at all. Hell, not that many friends."

They both nodded. "Maddox stepped in like he's known her all her life. Right now, he's like an uncle or older brother. But it's all too easy to imagine it blossoming into something more. Something larger."

Abby put her head on her hands and looked at me dreamily. "That's so sweet," she whispered. "I knew he'd surprise you in the end."

Kara sighed. "There's just something about the Kingston men."

Abby and I both nodded as we watched our food approach. Once we had our plates in front of us, Abby started telling us about something ultra-romantic Jury had done for her.

My phone beeped halfway through her story, and though I didn't want to be rude to my friend, it was the tone that indicated Maddox was trying to get in touch with me. No way I could resist checking.

You having fun with your friends?

I smiled and typed a quick reply. **I am. I've been neglecting them.**

He didn't reply, so I slipped my phone back in my purse. Seconds later, the back of my neck prickled. I turned to look behind me and desire slammed through me when I spotted Maddox greeting diners as he worked his way toward our table. Damn, but he wore that uniform well. Very, very well.

Kara turned to see what I was looking at. As soon as she realized Maddox was heading our way, she giggled and slid out of the booth. Abby scooted over and Kara sat beside her and dragged her plate across.

"Hello, ladies." He greeted Abby and Kara with a nod and smile before his eyes landed on me. "Bethany."

The way my name rolled off his tongue made my skin crawl with anticipation. I knew exactly what he was capable of doing with that mouth. And those hands. And... other parts. "Maddox," I whispered.

He leaned over, never breaking our gaze. I lifted my face upward to maintain the eye contact, and when his lips met mine in front of the whole diner, my nipples pebbled under my bra as shivers coursed through my body. The diner went silent because of course most eyes were on Maddox. He was a police officer in uniform, which would've attracted attention either way, but on top of that, he was the youngest Kingston. Black Claw royalty.

Our first PDA. Wow.

And once again, I thanked the inventors of the lightly padded bra.

He straightened up with a self-satisfying and smug expression on his face, but it didn't bother me. I felt pretty damn smug myself. I'd never felt this way about anyone else in my entire life. What was a little PDA when my emotions were so strong?

"Sit?" I asked and gestured toward the empty space in the booth beside me.

He shook his head. "No, I'm on patrol. I just wanted to stop in and ask you if you'd come to a cookout at my family's place on Saturday." He glanced at his smartwatch. "Er, tomorrow."

Abby grunted and swallowed her sip of tea. "Yeah, Jury mentioned it to me," she exclaimed. "You should come!"

A family gathering seemed like an enormous step, but with both Maddox and Abby grinning at me like a couple of fools, plus Kara nodding her head enthusiastically, how could I have said no? Besides, we'd slept together. Surely meeting his family wasn't all that big of a step, was it?

As I nodded my head, I was surprised to find I actually wanted to go. I was curious about what his mother was like. I'd seen her around but never officially met her.

"Okay," I said softly and tucked my hair behind my ear. "That sounds nice."

"Bring Tiffany," Maddox said. My heart swelled. "My family loves kids. It'll be like having a babysitter for her, I promise."

He wanted Tiffany to come, too. It wasn't just me meeting his family, it was his family meeting us. The significance was not lost on me. Not at all.

With a final kiss, Maddox said goodbye to the three of us and worked his way out of the diner, saying goodbye to all the people he'd greeted when he arrived.

As soon as he was out of earshot, Kara let out a tiny squeal. "I'm so excited for you!"

My chest fluttered with anticipation. "Oh, my gosh," I whispered. "What am I going to wear?"

***

The next day, true to their word, Kara and Abby showed up early to go through my closet. By the time Maddox arrived, I'd tried on about forty outfits and we landed on artfully ripped jeans, a flowy blouse covered in small pink roses, and ballet flats that matched the color of the roses. Abby helped me craft my makeup so it looked natural while Kara put a few extra curls in my hair—up in a ponytail that to most would look casual and quickly done.

Kara checked her watch. "He'll be here any minute," she squealed. "Let's go!"

Tiffany had helped us every step of the way. She'd been the one to pick out the shirt. After my outfit was ready, she'd insisted we all go to her room and help her pick one. She made the choices, of course, landing on her favorite play outfit with princesses on the front of the tee, as I'd known she would.

It didn't matter what she wore. They'd love her; everyone did. I did put my foot down and make her sit still so Kara could fix her hair and put in a floppy bow. I did love her with a bow in her hair, though it'd be lost before she met everyone.

Oh, well. The first impression would be good, at least.

Kara and Abby left seconds before Maddox turned onto my road. I slammed the door shut so he wouldn't realize I'd been waiting by the door with bated breath.

Darting into Tiffany's room, I flitted around and waited for the doorbell to ring. "Mommy?" Tiffany cocked her head at me. "Whatcha doin'?"

"Nothing, sweetie. Just waiting for a second."

The doorbell saved me from having to answer. Tiffany ran out and to the door, so I had to scramble to catch up to her. "Ask who it is," I hissed before she could yank the door open.

"Who is it?" she called.

"It's Maddox!"

Tiffany jerked the door open with a squeal. "Maddoth!"

He held out his arms and she launched into them. "I'm happy to see you, too, pipsqueak." His grin melted my heart, even more when he turned his big hazel eyes to me. "You ready?"

His gaze burned into me intently, then raked up and down my body. "You look great."

The weight of his gaze made my spine tingle. "Thanks," I whispered. "I'm ready."

I grabbed my purse and keys. "We can drive my car since Tiffany's car seat is already in there," I suggested.

He nodded and swung her around on the front walk while I locked the door. "Sounds good!"

Every mile closer to his family's home made my stomach clench tighter and tighter. He showed me where to turn and within fifteen minutes, we were there.

Maddox took my hand and squeezed while Tiffany unbuckled her belt. "Ready?" His grin could've lit up a room. "They're going to love you." He must've sensed my nerves. "Don't be scared." He looked a little sad for a moment. "My family is pretty cool."

"What's wrong?" I asked.

"Sometimes I forget how lucky I am to have the family I do," he said. He jumped out of the car and opened the back door for Tiff, then waited at the front of the car to take my hand before leading us up the stairs and into the enormous manor house.

Without giving me time to marvel at the big foyer or all the dark wood, Maddox pulled me into an empty living room. "Where is everyone?" I wondered in a hushed voice. The living room looked more like a library or study, except huge. It also had multiple couches and chairs and a big television on one wall. More like a den-library-living room. We carried on, out another door into a big kitchen with a very long table and huge island.

A woman turned from the stove. "Maddox," she said. "There you are."

She smiled warmly at me. "Bethany," Maddox said. "This is my grandmother, Carla. Nana, this is Bethany."

Tiffany clung to my leg. She was always a little bit shy for the first thirty seconds of meeting someone. "And who is this?" Carla bent over and smiled. "You must be the famous Tiffany."

Tiff nodded.

"Would you like to help me take food out?" Carla asked. "I have a lot of cookies to carry."

That was all it took for Tiffany to overcome her shyness. She darted forward eagerly. "I love cookies."

Carla laughed. "I thought you might."

Maddox pulled gently so I followed him out the back door. And there were all the people. The loud, boisterous talking and laughing stopped when we exited the building. "Hello," Maddox said. "Everyone, this is Bethany."

Tiffany appeared behind me with a plate of cookies and wide eyes. "And this is Tiffany," Maddox continued.

A little girl, barely a teenager, with long dark hair, ran forward. "Hi," she said. "I'm Maddox's sister, Hailey. Is it okay if I play with Tiffany?"

I nodded and smiled my thanks, and it turned out Maddox had been right. That was the last I had to worry about my daughter all day. Hailey fawned over her and made sure she was taken care of, as did Carla.

The next person to approach us was Maddox's mother. I knew her on sight, but we'd never been formally introduced. "Bethany, this is my mother, Ava. Mom, this is Bethany. She's..." He stared at me for a split second. "She's special."

Ava pulled me into a hug. "It's wonderful to meet you." She had an awful lot of emotion in her voice for someone just meeting a girl her son was dating.

"Hey, Maddox, come here!" Jury yelled across the yard. "We need one more for touch football."

Maddox squeezed my arm. "I'll leave you ladies to get to know each other."

I was a bit aggravated at him for abandoning me for a second, but Abby appeared as soon as he ran off. "Hey!" she said brightly. "Anybody you need to be introduced to?"

I looked around at all the people, and Maddox's mom put her arm around me. "You know my husband, Maverick?"

"I met him once at a police department supper," I said. "It's been years."

"Well, he's out there playing anyway. I'll introduce the women. Charlotte," she called. A gorgeous blonde looked up with a toddler on her hip. "Come meet Maddox's girlfriend."

I didn't know if we were at the boyfriend-girlfriend stage, but I wasn't about to argue that with Maddox's mother.

The blonde walked across the back deck. "So nice to meet you." She shifted the baby to the other hip and held out her hand for me to shake. "I'm a nurse at the hospital, so if you ever need anything, you just let me know, okay?"

I nodded. "Thank you. It's always nice to have medical friends."

She giggled and gestured to another woman who had just walked up. Ava smiled. "Bethany, this is—"

"Oh, I know Bethany," Harley exclaimed. As Abby's sister, we'd ended up at more than one girls' night together.

"Good to see you, Harley. I didn't know you were related to the Kingstons, other than through Abby," I said.

Harley pointed toward the field. "The dark-haired man with glasses is my fiancé, Stefan."

"From the body shop?" I asked. He'd changed my spark plugs a few months before.

Harley nodded. "He's sort of adopted into the Kingston family."

"That's nice," I said warmly. They all seemed so kind. I couldn't help but wonder what it would be like to be a part of such a large family.

"Okay, everyone!" Carla yelled behind me, making me jump. "Come eat!"

The back yard had several tables set up, one of which was covered with food. Everything from hot dogs to steaks. Potato salad and watermelon, and some sort of fried vegetable that looked Southern and wonderful.

Maddox ran up with a light sheen of sweat on his forehead. "Let's eat."

He and I circled the table, loading up our plates, but he did it with one hand on my back as if he couldn't stand to stop touching me.

I didn't mind it one bit. Everyone kept me talking all through the meal, and I found myself telling them about my business, about Tiffany—leaving out the more tragic aspects of her past—and even about upcoming projects. I learned about Ava's online business, Harley's salon—hello invitation for free services! Yes!

The day passed quickly with a lot of laughter and fun. By the time Tiffany began to yawn, I was content with just being around those wonderful people. They fully supported and loved one another. I couldn't help but think how nice it could be to marry into the Kingston family.

But it was far, far too soon to think about that.

Chapter 16 - Maddox

Our dinner had gone well. My entire family loved Bethany, and unless I was much mistaken, she loved them, too.

We'd just gotten back to her house, and Tiffany had fallen asleep nearly as soon as we hit my grandparents' driveway. Bethany carried her to bed while I waited in the living room. I hoped she was going to invite me to stay.

When she walked back into the living room, I held my arms out. Her smile warmed me as she wrapped her arms around my waist, and I hugged her close. She lifted her head so I could press a kiss to her lips. "I'm so happy with how this night went," I whispered. "I knew they'd love you."

Bethany beamed at me. "I was so nervous, but it was like I'd been a part of their crowd all my life." She tucked her head into the crook of my neck. "Thank you."

We stayed there for a few moments, then she blinked up at me with something in her eyes I hoped was desire. "Come on," she whispered. "Come to bed."

Hell, yes. I followed her to her bedroom, my eyes trained to her ass as she seemed to sashay—no, float—across the floor. I could barely believe this woman belonged to me. I was truly the luckiest guy in the world.

She closed the door behind us and smiled at me. The shyest, softest smile I'd ever seen. It was like being in a dream.

"Are you shy?" I tucked a length of hair behind her ear and smoothed her cheek. "Afraid?"

"Not afraid." She shook her head. "Anticipation?"

"You don't need to be shy, either. It's just me." Moonlight fell through the window, lighting her face, and her pupils were huge as she looked at me. Then she turned and walked across the room to lower the blinds, flicking soft lamps on as she passed them.

In just a few moments, she'd set the stage for romance, for love, and Artemis almost purred in satisfaction. Yes, he loved this human too. That's why he chose her.

"I feel like I should have brought you something." I scrubbed my hand across my head.

She chuckled. "Brought me something like what? Happiness? You already did that."

A rush of pleasure warmed my whole body, and Artemis shifted, making himself comfortable. He was at ease tonight, restful.

"No. Like flowers." The idea sounded dumb as soon as I voiced it. "Chocolates, maybe."

"I don't need anything like that." She walked slowly toward me before stopping right in front of me. "You said you wanted to show me something?"

I sucked a deep breath and nodded.

"I've already seen it," she blurted, ruining the solemn moment, but I laughed as she clapped her hand over her mouth.

"Maybe I'd like to show you again sometime."

"I'd like that." She hooked her fingers into my belt loops and drew me closer until my hips sat flush with her body.

I looked down, my gaze landing on her skin, her eyes, her lips, and her mouth parted as I watched, her breaths coming as soft pants. The temptation was too much, and I bowed my head, leaning into her.

Our lips met and hers were so soft, and her tongue slid against mine with a mixture of innocence and passion. Before I fell too far under, before I all but drowned in her, I moved back a little.

Her eyes flicked open, her startled gaze meeting mine.

I rested my forehead against hers and swallowed, suddenly anxious. It skittered through me, scraping along my nerves like unwanted sand in my ass-crack after a day at the beach. I closed my eyes. That was a dumb thought right before I spoke to Beth.

I took another deep breath, and Bethany parted her lips like she was going to speak, but I couldn't let her say anything until I did.

"I love you, Bethany." For a moment, the words hung in the air between us, fragile and easily dismissed.

I waited with my breath tight in my chest.

"I love you, too." Her voice was so quiet I should have had to strain to hear her, but even Artemis heard, and an intense growl of ownership vibrated through my chest.

I swept her back into my arms, lifting her to me and cradling her to my chest, right against my heart. It beat faster, wildly almost, but I didn't want to excite Artemis, so I drew a calming breath.

Now wasn't about my dragon. Now was about showing Beth my love. My devotion. How I'd utterly fallen for her in the few short weeks since I'd met her, even though I resisted it at first.

I laid her on her bed. "I love you," I said again as I shed my clothes and climbed up beside her. "I'd like to show you how much."

She nodded, the moment slow and almost uncertain like she'd caught that my tempo was leisurely and more serious. But then she sat up and tugged her dress up her body to take it off, revealing delicate lace underwear with small stitched flowers.

I skimmed my hand across her abdomen. One day, hopefully, my baby would grow in there. Her muscles fluttered delicately under her skin at my touch, and I smiled before pressing a kiss over each of the movements.

She lay back down with her head on her pillows, and I glanced up her body, between her breasts to meet her gaze as she watched me. Then, I lowered my head again and kissed a path to her mouth. Her arms wound around me, holding me close, and I kissed her slowly, reverently, worshiping her with my lips and tongue.

I skimmed a hand across her breasts and lowered the thin straps to create the room to slide my fingers inside, where I could touch her hardening nipples. She gasped a little, and I lowered my head, flicking my tongue across the lace and sucking her nipple through the fabric.

When she wriggled and reached around her back to take her bra off, I chuckled. "It doesn't matter what speed I go, you're always impatient." But as her bra slackened, I drew it away from her body to lay her bare to me and swirled my tongue across her sensitive skin. She pushed her fingers into my hair, and her breath came in pants as she moved her hips, writhing slowly.

I slipped my hand down her waist and played with the band of her panties where it sat against her skin.

"Yes." She breathed the word, and it was all the permission I needed.

I followed the fabric down and pressed my fingers between her thighs. She widened her legs in answer and arched toward me.

"You're already so wet." I could feel it through the lace.

"Because I want you." She arched again, pushing herself to me.

A rush of love for her filled my chest, and Artemis stirred before settling again, safe in the knowledge we were loving our woman.

I drew her panties down, and nuzzled her thighs, kissing the skin and breathing her scent. When I kissed closer, higher, she shifted away.

"No. Not there. I want you inside me."

"Just one taste…" I was so close, but I watched for her reaction first.

She nodded, and lapped my tongue against her, taking it over her clit and listening to her breathing rate change.

"Please, Maddox."

That was all it took, the sound of my name on her lips, and I shifted over her, maintaining the contact between our bodies as I moved. Awareness of her prickled through me, and my hard cock brushed over her thigh. The heaviness of it excited me.

I dropped another kiss on her breast, taking things slowly, teasing her a little. Teasing myself too, because I wanted her, but I also wanted to hold back. I wanted to love her instead of just fuck her.

I moved my hips, stroking the underside of my shaft against her leg, and the skin of my cock tightened as I hardened further.

Artemis huffed a sigh. He didn't understand the difference between fucking our mate and loving her when arousal stoked our desire, but as I nestled myself between Beth's legs, I captured her lips for another slow kiss.

I slid my tongue into her mouth, tasting her, stroking her, and she responded, drawing heat through me until my skin almost burned at her delicate touch.

"I'm ready." She pressed against me, and I nudged forward, pushing the head of my cock into her wet heat.

But I didn't want to go too fast. I wanted to enjoy this and prolong her pleasure, too.

I drew out, waiting a moment before pushing back in, and she sighed as she surrendered herself to me. Her head dropped to one side, and I sucked gently at the skin on her neck, passing my tongue over the vein beneath the surface that throbbed with the beat of her heart.

My heart beat for her, and I wanted to show her that.

I kept my movements slow, entering her and retreating until she accepted my whole length inside her, and I paused for a moment to allow her to accommodate me comfortably.

When she began to move beneath me, her hips pressing to mine, I mimicked her, picking up her rhythm as I shared her body.

"It's an honor." I voiced the thought quietly, and Artemis scoffed a quiet rumble, but he understood. We were lucky.

"Hmm?" Beth sounded distracted, and I sure the hell hoped she was because I was pretty sure I was nudging her just right.

"I love you." I couldn't say it enough.

She looked at me, her beautiful eyes framed by impossibly long eyelashes and smiled. "I love you, too." Then she cupped the back of my head. "Kiss me."

I probed her with my tongue again, matching the rhythm to my cock, and she gasped as her breathing became fractured. She let out a low moan as she tensed, and her fingers clenched around my arm before she throbbed around me, sending wave after wave of sensation to my balls and they tightened.

I drew a last inhale and held it as I hit the point of no return. Then all thoughts left my mind and I came in a shuddering gasp as sensation pulsed in waves over me.

As small sparks still ran through me, interrupting my ability to breathe, I nudged my still-hard cock in her, ignoring the sensitivity in it.

"Thank you," I whispered, awe for her coloring my tone.

She grinned lazily, stretching beneath me. "No, thank you, my love."

"I do love you." I said it again, in case she'd forgotten and kissed her forehead, then the tip of her nose, and finally her lips.

This was exactly where I was supposed to be.

Chapter 17 - Bethany

Sunday marked something else I'd never done before. I let Maddox spend the night so that when Tiffany woke, Maddox was already here. I woke early and made pancakes and sausage, Tiffany's favorite. Maddox shuffled out of my bedroom in his jeans and T-shirt, looking rumpled.

Tiffany came down the hall at almost the same time. Her face went from sleepy to delighted when she spotted Maddox. "Maddoth!" She ran to give him a hug around the knees. "What are you doing here?"

"Well," he said, then looked at me for guidance.

I opted for the truth. "Maddox stayed the night," I said.

Tiffany nodded and didn't seem to really care. "What's for breakfast? I'm hungry."

At nearly four, her sentences were pretty clear, with only her slight lisp which was so cute I almost hated for her to outgrow it. "Pancakes and sausage!"

Maddox cheered with Tiffany. I gave him a quizzical look.

He shrugged. "I love pancakes and sausage."

The rest of the day sped by so fast. Almost too fast. Maddox had to leave after lunch for the late shift at the police department.

Monday morning, I took Tiffany to my mom's, where she ran off without even saying goodbye to find her Papaw. Mom handed me a cup of coffee. "Spill."

After a long talk with my mom about Maddox and the Kingstons, I felt even better about how the weekend had gone. As Mom said, what was life without a few risks?

On my way back to the office to get a bit of work done, I got a call from the lawyer Maddox had recommended. He'd asked me to send over all the information I had, and I'd sent it early the week before. "Could you come down to the office?" he asked. "It shouldn't take long."

"Of course." I thanked him and hung up, then immediately dialed Maddox. "Hey, the lawyer wants to meet."

"Want me to go with you?" He offered immediately and without hesitation.

"If you're free, I'd appreciate it so much. I just dropped Tiffany off at my parents' house."

"Swing by and pick me up. I'm off today."

I promised to be there soon and hung up, then pulled back out onto the road. Maddox waited at the curb in the parking lot of his apartment complex and hopped in. "I'm sure it's good news," he said.

"You're probably right, but I can't help but be nervous." I sighed and turned the car around toward the lawyer's office. He worked in the next town over, which wasn't a long drive. His office was near the hospital Charlotte worked at.

We chatted about some silly call Maddox had taken the night before. It helped calm my nerves so that by the time we got there, I was only half a basket case instead of full-blown.

We only had to wait in the receptionist's office for a few minutes before she led us back to an inner office. "Ms. Leeds, welcome. I'm Colton Kennedy, we spoke on the phone." A tall black man held out his hand and smiled warmly. "Maddox, nice to see you again." He shook both our hands and gestured for us to sit down.

"Thank you for taking my case," I said. He was the most popular lawyer in the area, according to Maddox.

"Well, I had a chance to look over your statements and everything. Your financials are in order. I got the statement from your parents and witnesses." He spread his hands out. "They don't have a case." My heart soared. I hadn't really thought they had, but it was wonderful to hear the words spoken out loud by a real lawyer.

With a chuckle, he closed the folder laid out on the desk in front of him. "There's no proof of negligence. I got a statement from Tiffany's pediatrician's office as well." He shrugged. "At best, once a DNA test proves they are Tiffany's paternal grandparents, they can file for visitation, which you can fight."

I nodded. "I know Walter drinks and is pretty controlling with Mary, and was very controlling with Kyle when he was a child. But besides being completely cowed by Walter, Mary was a good mother to Kyle. That's what he always told me."

Colton nodded, and Maddox sort of stayed in the background with his fingers threaded through mine. He was mainly there for moral support, and I appreciated it. Even more that he didn't try to interfere or make it about him. He was only here for me. "I don't know about visitation," I said. "They don't know her. I wouldn't want to drop her off with them the way I do my parents."

"If they try for visitation, we'll make sure it's supervised. The state respects grandparents' rights, but they give the mother's opinions and statements heavy regard."

I nodded gratefully. "Thank you so much."

We finished up the last of his questions for me and shook his hand again. "Don't stress. I'm confident about a positive outcome. I'll call you with a date for mediation."

When we got in the car, I breathed a huge sigh of relief. "Wow." I looked at Maddox and shook my head. "I'm so glad to get that news."

He laughed. "Not to be one to say I told you so, but I told you! They don't stand a chance."

"Thank you for being there for me." I grabbed his hand and squeezed it between both of mine. "And for the lawyer recommendation and everything."

He put his fingertip on the bottom of my chin, so I tilted my face upward. Then, Maddox lowered his lips to mine and pressed a firm, possessive kiss there. "I told you. I'm here for you. I'd do anything for you."

I looked deep into his eyes and saw a surprising amount of devotion there. We'd both said we were falling for each other, and I knew I meant it. But I'd figured he was just caught up in the passion and his feelings had been strong. But it wasn't just passion. There was an intense devotion in his gaze that I couldn't ignore.

His other hand rose to my face and he cupped my cheeks. "I love you, Bethany. I'm in love with you."

My heart thudded in my chest so loud I was sure he could hear it, too. My mind fuzzed and all I knew was Maddox.

"You don't have to say it," he continued when I didn't respond. He thought I hesitated because I didn't feel it.

It wasn't that. I was just overwhelmed with emotions. I swallowed the lump in my throat and mimicked Maddox by putting my hands on his face. "I love you, too," I whispered.

I dropped Maddox back at his place to get ready for an afternoon hiking with his cousins. Apparently, they were outdoorsy. I'd planned to hike myself, but he didn't invite me, so I figured I'd go off on the trail I liked and get some alone time. The day was shot for trying to focus on work, anyway.

After a brisk hike and picking Tiffany up, I made an easy dinner and we went to bed. Tuesday passed in a blur of texting Maddox, who had a long shift at the station and dealing with plans for the new property.

Wednesday after I dropped Tiffany off at my parents' house, I settled in at my desk and my cell phone rang. I checked the call log to find Kyle's mom's cell phone number. "Not today, Mary. The lawyer said not to talk to you." I rejected the call and moved on with my day. Finally, it was nice to feel like I didn't have to answer when they called. It was probably Walter on Mary's phone, anyway, trying to fool me into picking up so he could rant at me some more.

But Colton had said any conversation with them before the mediation was a no-go. I carried on with my day with a weight off my shoulders. They couldn't get to me anymore and the weekly calls would hopefully end soon. I'd asked Colton to make that a stipulation in the mediation. If they wanted supervised visitation, they had to stop calling me, especially when Walter was drunk.

Things were finally looking up. I felt like a million bucks as I made a to-do list for the new property.

My phone beeped the special tune for Maddox, and I picked it up eagerly. **Lunch at the diner?**

I replied as fast as I could. **Be right there.**

Then, I let Kara know when I'd be back. We were supposed to meet up soon to go over plans.

Lunch at the diner with Maddox was a dream. I couldn't have said afterward what I ate. All I remembered was sitting down across from him and the feel of his thumb stroking across my knuckles as we ate and stared at each other. We talked about little nonsense, like favorite colors and our least favorite movies.

The kind of conversations new relationships were full of. The wonderful, getting-to-know each other sort. The short date put a smile on my face I couldn't shake. It stayed with me until I saw Mom when I picked up Tiffany. Her face was like a storm cloud.

"What's wrong?" I asked. Something definitely was, I just didn't know what.

"Since when do Kyle's parents call here?" she asked.

My blood boiled. "They're probably freaking out because they realize they don't have a case and they aren't going to do anything with this suit but waste their money."

"I thought you said it was all handled?" Mom asked. "I'm not upset with you, honey, but I'm upset that they'd go to such lengths to get in touch with you."

They'd never bothered my parents before. Why now? I wanted to call and tell them where they could shove it, but the lawyer wouldn't like that one bit, I was sure. "If they call again, make a note. Write down the date and time and anything they say. I'll give it to the lawyer, and it'll help our case." I gave Mom a sympathetic look. "I'm sorry."

It had to be because I didn't answer. I'd never told my mom or dad that Walter and Mary called me so frequently about Kyle's death. It would've worried them when I understood why they did it. They'd lost a child. Could I really blame them for needing someone to blame? "I'll handle it, okay?"

"Is this normal?" Mom asked. "Have they called you before?"

I evaded the question by walking toward the living room when I heard Tiffany. "How's Tiff? Have a good day?"

"Yes. You didn't answer my question."

I sighed and turned back to my mother. "Mary calls me occasionally, but she only wants to reminisce and talk about Kyle. Walter calls about once a week. He's usually drunk, and he blames me for everything, repeatedly."

Mom's face fell. "Oh, Bethany. Honey." She wrapped her arms around me. "Why didn't you tell me?"

"Tell you what?" My dad came out of the living room with a concerned look on his face. "What's wrong?"

I repeated what I'd told mom. Dad's face turned into a thundercloud. "I ought to go show Walter what for."

"Dad, come on, no. They lost their son. They didn't handle it well, but I try to be sympathetic. They're hurting."

"It's been years. It's time to place blame where blame is due, and that's squarely at Kyle's feet," Mom said.

I shushed her and nodded my head toward Tiffany, who was on the couch doing a puzzle.

Mom nodded and lowered her voice. "They are wrong for calling and blaming you. Kyle made the choice to drive the way he did. He made the choice to try to pressure you into a relationship you didn't want."

"I know, Mom. And that's why I put it into the mediation." I explained my clause. They seemed to look a bit mollified at that news.

Mom stepped forward again and put her hands on my shoulders. "Honey, you should've told us years ago. You're not alone in this world. We're here for you."

My dad put his arm around my shoulders. "Bethany, Tiffany is about to turn four. In the last four years, nearly five since you got pregnant, you've been a superwoman. You need to allow others to help you. Let us do more."

"I already bring Tiffany here all the time for you to keep," I pointed out. "What more?"

"Let Maddox keep helping," Mom suggested. "I'm so glad you let him give you advice about the lawyer and let him go with you. It's so unlike you." She was right. It was very unlike me, but like she was, I was so thankful that I had.

"We'll report any more calls we get, okay?" Mom said. "Keep us posted if you get any, as well."

I promised, and Tiffany and I managed to get on our way.

"Mommy?" Tiffany said in the car.

"Yes, sweetheart?"

"Can we have pasketti for dinner?"

I thought about what I had in the cabinets. "We don't have everything we need for spaghetti; would you settle for lasagna?" I was pretty sure I had a frozen lasagna.

She sniffled, but said, "Yes."

That little sniffle was more than I could take. "I guess we can stop in the grocery store and get spaghetti noodles."

I looked at her little face in the rearview mirror. She lit up when I told her we'd go to the grocery store. Mostly because I almost always let her pick out a treat while we were there.

She made it through most of the store before spotting a pack of snack cakes she loved. I let her get them. Of course.

On the way out the door, I looked up and spotted Maddox's mom walking in. "Hello, Ava," I said warmly. She'd been so lovely at the cookout.

"Bethany and Tiffany!" Ava looked truly happy to see us. "How are you?"

"I got cakes!" Tiffany exclaimed. She held out her grocery bag. She'd had to have one just for her cakes, of course.

"Those look so good." Ava tweaked her on the nose and stood. "I'm glad to run into you. I'd like to invite the two of you to have dinner with us. Saturday night. Bring Tiffany, please. Hailey has been bugging me to have her over since the moment you left the manor."

Ava's approval was important to me, and the way she spoke to me told me she was genuinely happy to see me. It made my heart glow. "We would love to come," I said. "Please, let us bring something. The salad or the dessert?"

She waved her hand. "My Nana would roll over in her grave if I let my guest bring food. How about a bottle of wine?"

I clasped my hands together and beamed. "Perfect." I didn't know jack diddly about how to pick out a wine, but I trusted the clerk at the liquor store to help me.

After getting home, as I finished the spaghetti dishes, Maddox's voice rang across the living room. "Hello?"

Tiffany ran screaming out of her room and launched herself into Maddox's arms. "We're going to eat dinner at your mommy's house!"

Maddox looked at me quizzically over her head. "We ran into your mom at the grocery store and she invited us to dinner Saturday night."

His face broke into a big grin. "That means she likes you. She only feeds the people she likes."

I sighed in relief. "I'm glad to hear that. She's such a nice person."

He snorted. "She's had her moments. But I'm glad she likes you, because I'm planning to keep you around for a while, and it'll be much easier if you two get along."

Tiffany wiggled in his arms, so he set her down. She ran back to her room, already over the thrill of her Maddoth coming over.

"Besides." He held out his arms, and I gladly stepped into his embrace. "There's something I want to tell you. Saturday, after dinner. If we're going to continue with this relationship, I want to be perfectly honest with you about me and my life."

My heart instantly squeezed with worry. What had he kept from me? Was he married? Used to be a woman? I could deal with that, but it would've been a shock. Married was a no-go, of course.

"No, don't look worried," he said, speaking quickly. "It's okay. I just want us to start our relationship on an open, honest plane."

That didn't do much to quell my fears. He pressed a kiss to my forehead. "Really. It's all going to be fine."

I opted to believe him since he'd never given me a reason to doubt him. But it didn't make me less nervous.

Chapter 18 - Maddox

As soon as I walked into Bethany's house on Saturday evening, I knew something was wrong. She was visibly upset. "What's wrong?"

Artemis went on high alert. We'd been worried about telling her our secret, but something else was going on. I had to figure out what and fix it if possible.

She rolled her eyes. "More calls from Kyle's parents."

They must be stopped.

Artemis was right. "You need to let me serve them with a restraining order," I suggested. "Have you been reporting the calls to your lawyer?"

Bethany gave me a flat look. "Of course. And they are harmless, if persistent. I don't need a restraining order."

I didn't want to argue with her, so I tried to let it go. "Okay. You ready?"

She nodded. "Almost. I just need to grab Tiffany's shoes."

Tiffany followed Bethany out of the room. I waited patiently, or at least I tried to. Artemis kept bugging me to protect Bethany and Tiffany.

"You could change your number," I said.

Bethany stopped in her tracks with Tiff's shoes in her hand. "Maddox, stop. I don't need you to constantly suggest what I should and shouldn't do."

"I don't mean to overstep. I'm sorry. It was just an idea." I knew she didn't like being told what to do, but I thought our relationship had progressed to the point that I could be an active member of her life. "Hang on." I held up a finger. "Why are we in a place where I can tell you I love you and you can tell me, and we're thinking about building a life together, but I can't make suggestions without you getting angry with me?"

She stared at me for several seconds before responding. "I'm not used to someone telling me what to do like I'm a child."

Never did I think she was a child. "That's not what I did. Not at all. I'm a cop, and I want to be a lawyer. And I'm your..." *Mate*, but I couldn't say that. "Boyfriend or whatever we are, and it's my responsibility to protect you."

Her eyes narrowed. "Responsibility? Why isn't it my responsibility to protect you?" She tossed her hair as if she'd made some big point.

"Because I'm a *cop*," I exclaimed.

Tiffany ran into the room. "Are you fighting?"

"No," Bethany said sharply. "We're having a conversation."

Tiffany didn't buy it, but she sat on the couch and stuck her feet out. "Shoes, Mommy. I want to go see Ava."

Bethany sat beside her. "Maddox, I'm a strong, independent woman. I've relied on myself for a long time, and I've been relying on you too much. I don't *need* a man to do anything for me."

"You may not need me to, but isn't it nice to share the responsibilities with someone?" I pointed out. "I want to help. I want to be a part of your life. Why is that so galling for you?"

She took a deep breath and patted Tiffany's leg. "Let's drop this for now and go have dinner."

Well, at least that was a good sign. She didn't want to cancel or break up because we were having one argument.

Although, if we were this upset over one argument, what would happen when it was something bigger? Only time would tell, but it didn't bode well for us.

Stop upsetting her. This is a big day.

I'd been so excited about today. I was going to tell Bethany about Artemis. I hadn't meant to upset her. And Artemis kept going back and forth. I couldn't protect her without upsetting her, apparently.

Why were women so confusing?

Tiffany chattered all the way to my parents' house, helping break the tension up a bit. We talked to her and smiled at each other. I knew we'd figure this all out, but the night had a bit of a sour tint to it now. I just wished she'd stop fighting me at every turn.

Bethany drove, and Tiffany's car seat was behind the passenger seat, so when she parked the car in my parents' driveway, I hopped out and got Tiffany out. She'd fallen asleep on the drive. She held up her arms, a little shy. I'd noticed it took her a few minutes to warm up, but once she did, she was a firecracker.

I picked her up and was again reminded that if I decided to go to California, I wouldn't just lose Bethany, I'd lose Tiffany, too. Probably, Bethany and I would reconnect later. That was the nature of mates. But I'd never gain the same trust and relationship with Tiffany when she was older.

My attachment to both of them had grown pretty damn strong. I really loved them. As Tiffany clung to my neck and went back to sleep with her head on my shoulder, I hugged her and waited for Bethany to catch up. Today wasn't about California, anyway. The more time went by, the less I wanted to go. Today was about Artemis and

Bethany. The other stuff would work out, one way or another.

I'd decided to tell Bethany about Artemis with my family around, so she'd have support from people who had already been through this. It was one hell of a shock when I found out, and I had Artemis inside me to help me. It had to be beyond difficult for the mates of dragons.

Tiffany was totally wiped. "She didn't nap today," Bethany said. "She was too excited."

I tapped on the door, then opened it and stuck my head in. My mother pulled the door open the rest of the way. "Hello," she cried, then clapped her hand over her mouth when she spotted Tiffany. "Take her to the guest room," she whispered. "You and your father can listen for her."

But I was already heading up the stairs. That was exactly what I'd planned to do, anyway.

Tiffany fluttered her eyes when I laid her down, but she muttered my name and rolled onto her side. After covering her with a blanket, I turned to see Bethany had followed me. "Hey," I whispered.

"Hey." She looked at me with big, vulnerable eyes. This wasn't going to be an easy night for her.

"Can we pretend we didn't fight and have a good night?" I asked. "We'll find a balance where you let me help you some, but I don't overstep."

She nodded and stepped forward. I took that as a cue to gather her into my arms and press a kiss to the top of her head. "Starting a relationship isn't easy," she said into my shoulder.

"No, it's not. And I don't have any experience with committed relationships. I've only ever dated casually." That was something I'd been embarrassed to admit before.

But she chuckled. "Same here. Kyle was my most committed relationship, but he was my best friend who I only had sex with once. I'm not exactly what you'd call a relationship expert."

"At least we're newbs together," I joked. "Come on. Let's go eat."

As we headed down the stairs, she stopped suddenly. "With our argument, I forgot the wine. I told your mom I'd bring the wine."

With a chuckle, I tugged on her arm. "If I know my mom, she forgot all about that."

We walked down the hall and entered the kitchen to find Mom placing dishes on the table and Dad setting out silverware. "We thought we'd eat in here," Mom said. "It's more intimate and casual."

Bethany nodded, but then turned to my mom. "Ava, I'm so sorry. Maddox and I were talking when we left, and I walked right out without the wine."

My mother touched Bethany's arm. "Honey, it's fine. I've got plenty. I prefer if my guests don't bring anything, anyway." She squeezed her arm, then hurried away to get the rest of the food on the table.

"Hello," Hailey said brightly from the table. "I can't wait for Tiffany to wake up!"

"You'll wait just fine," Mom said. "Boys, if you want to go out back and make sure the steaks are ready. They should be about done."

"Can I help?" Bethany asked.

Mom didn't want anyone to bring anything, but she wasn't afraid to put us to work. "Sure," she said. "Here, cut up this tomato for the salad."

I followed Dad out onto the deck and the smell of the steaks hit me. "Bethany likes hers medium well," I said.

"We'll have to leave it on a bit longer with Hailey's and your mother's," he said. "Ours should be done. Rare."

Rare meat was a particular favorite of any dragon shifter. The dragons loved to hunt game for themselves, but as humans, we had a real preference for rare meat and never got an upset stomach.

"Are you ready for this?" Dad asked as he took our seared pieces of meat off the grill.

"It's time. I love her and I plan on keeping her in my life, so it has to be done, doesn't it? I mean, I'm not looking forward to it, but what choice do I have?" I held out the plate for the steaks.

Dad closed the grill to cook the ladies' steaks longer, then patted me on the shoulder. "It'll work out. I'm proud of you."

"Thanks, Dad."

We hung out on the deck a few more minutes until all the meat was done, then took it inside to rest.

Mom took over as soon as we came in, bustling around and making everyone sit. Before I knew it, I was crammed next to a blinking Tiffany, who had just woken up from her impromptu nap. Hailey sat on her other side, cutting up tiny bits of steak for her. Bethany kept looking around me to make sure Hailey did it right. "She's fine," I said, and winked to let her know I was teasing. "Relax and enjoy yourself."

I waited through the entire dinner. The more time went by, the more Bethany relaxed. I wanted her to be as at ease as possible before springing the news on her.

My parents were lifesavers. They kept her talking and laughing and by the time Mom brought out the pies, she was totally at ease. Too bad I was about to rip her right out of that comfort zone.

"Hailey, would you care to take Tiffany to your room and play?" I asked.

Hailey's face lit up. She knew what was going to happen, but she didn't care about seeing me shift. She'd seen it before, repeatedly. She cared more about getting to be a babysitter. "Sure!" she chirped. "Come on, Tiffany, do you want to play makeup?"

I glanced at Bethany, worried she'd disapprove of a thirteen-year-old putting makeup on a three-year-old, but she laughed. "She loves to play makeup."

One problem down. Now the big one. "Let's go onto the deck," Dad said. "Have a glass of wine."

We'd all had one with dinner, though Mom had filled Bethany's up every time she took a sip. It was a little obvious she was trying to get her tipsy, but I didn't think Beth had noticed.

Mom nodded eagerly. "That sounds lovely."

Bethany looked at me, but I grabbed both our glasses and followed my parents out, holding the door open with my foot for Bethany to follow.

"It is a nice night," Bethany said. Our summers came in late, so it wasn't exactly hot, but the chill was gone out of the air.

I handed Bethany her drink, then scooted a deck chair close to the one she sat in. "Bethany, there was a bigger purpose for us having dinner here tonight. There are some things about me that you should know before we go any further with our relationship."

She went from relaxed to high alert. I sensed her anxiety. "Why are we talking about this here, now?"

My mom scooted her chair closer. "Because I've been through this, too. I can help you."

Bethany tried not to bristle, but her spine straightened a bit.

"Bethany likes to be independent," I said. Maybe thinking she'd need help from my family to get through this had been the wrong idea. "But, Beth, I think it'll be good for Mom to be here while I tell you all about me. She's just like you, or she was once."

Mom nodded eagerly. "I know how you're going to be feeling, more than perhaps anyone alive. I had a daughter when Maverick and I got married. And she wasn't much older than Tiffany is now."

Bethany fixed me with a glare. "What is going on?"

"First, you need to know that I or my family would never hurt you or Tiffany. Not in a million years."

Her eyes widened. "What the hell are you people into? Mob? Some sort of gang?"

I shook my head and held up my hands, but Bethany recoiled. It was already going badly. "No, no, please, *please* try to keep an open mind. And remember, no matter what, that we'd never hurt you."

Just say it.

Artemis was right. "This is a part of who I am. It's half of me." I chuckled. "Sometimes it feels like all of me."

Bethany stared at me with wide eyes. I couldn't read her mind, of course, but it was obvious a million thoughts were racing.

"Bethany, I'm a dragon shifter. Like you might read about in novels or see in movies. I can shift into a dragon." Oh, man, that felt good to get off my chest.

Her wide eyes crinkled, and she burst out laughing. "Is this how you guys introduce someone into the family? With a practical joke?" She looked at each of us and her laughter faded. "It's not all that funny," she said lamely.

"It's not a joke, dear." My mother tried to touch Bethany's hand, but she jerked it away.

"You people are crazy. Actually mad. What makes you think this would be funny? Why would you joke like this?" Bethany's mood started to shift toward outrage and pure panic.

"This isn't a joke, Beth." I nodded toward my parents. They stood, and Bethany recoiled at their movement. She was freaked. They walked inside to give us a bit of privacy. I knew they'd come back out if I needed them. I waited until they shut the door to continue. "This is the truth, and I can show you, but you have to promise me you understand that I will not hurt you. My dragon, Artemis, won't hurt you. You are in absolutely zero danger."

She nodded her head.

She's about to bolt.

I stood and backed away, stepping down the stairs by feeling with my toes while I had my hands up. "Just don't run, okay? Give me time to show you, prove it, and explain. Promise you won't run."

She shook her head. "I'm not promising anything. You're freaking crazy."

There was nothing I could've done but show her. I intentionally wore the clothes I did for a quick change. No underwear, no undershirt, no socks. In seconds, I was naked. Bethany jumped up. "What are you doing?" she hissed.

"Just don't run!" That was the last thing I said before I let Artemis do his work. I encouraged him to shift quickly. In the late evening twilight, she wouldn't have been able to see the transition clearly, which could either help or hurt our cause.

As soon as Artemis was fully shifted, I smelled Bethany's fear. She was absolutely terrified. "No," she said. She backed up, hands up in front of her until she backed right into the house. "This isn't real."

Mom opened the back door, making Bethany jump. "It's okay," Mom said. "I went through this, too. I'm not a dragon. Only men can be."

"I'm hallucinating," she whispered.

"You're not," Mom said. "But it's okay to be freaked out. Everyone is when they first find out."

"Who?" she asked. "Who all is like this?"

Just the Kingston men. And Stefan. Artemis projected his thoughts into Ava's head, and she jumped with a little squeal.

"What was that?"

I am Artemis. I am Maddox's dragon. Or, Maddox is my human.

"How are you in my head?" she asked with honest terror in her voice.

You are our mate. I can communicate directly with you when shifted, and sometimes when Maddox is in his form if you open your mind enough.

"No." Bethany moaned and batted my mom's hand away again.

Please do not fear me. I would never hurt you.

Bethany continued to shake her head as the back door opened again. We all froze, shocked, as Tiffany came running out the back door. I heard Hailey calling her name.

"Dinosaur!" Tiffany screamed. But she wasn't afraid. She laughed and hurried forward, but in her excitement, she missed the stairs. Mom and Bethany lurched forward, but so did Artemis. He wanted to catch the little girl he loved as much as I did.

In his haste, he didn't retract his claws properly. He managed to catch her, but not without a long scratch up her arm. Tiffany recoiled and stumbled back up the four deck stairs, crying and screaming about the bad dinosaur. Bethany rushed forward, screaming for Artemis to get away from her daughter.

Artemis recoiled back into the yard and hung his head. Intense shame washed over both of us. He'd just been trying to help but made things exponentially worse.

What a disaster.

Chapter 19 - Bethany

I was completely losing my mind. Utterly disconnected from reality. Maybe I'd been drugged. Because there was no way dragons were real or that my boyfriend and his family were packed full of them.

As Tiffany ran toward me, I gathered her into my arms and yanked her as far back as I could. She held out her arm and showed me a scratch. It was shallow and slight, but long.

After he promised nobody would be hurt, that he and his family and his dragon—his *dragon*—would never hurt us, that was the first thing that had happened. I'd watched as the beast tried to grab Tiffany into his big, dangerous claws.

"This is unreal," I said, holding Tiffany close. "You said you're not dangerous," I yelled at the dragon.

I am not a danger to you.

Shaking my head, I blinked as if that could keep the creature from projecting his thoughts into my mind. "You obviously are. You tried to grab my daughter."

I tried to catch her. She was about to fall down the stairs.

How could I know if that was true?

"He won't hurt you," Ava said. "The dragons, they can be dangerous, of course. They can hunt and kill game, and they protect us. But he'd never intentionally cause you injury."

"He just did!" I pointed to Tiffany's arm. It had quit bleeding, but God only knew what sort of germs were in the cut from the dragon's claw. "I need to tend to her arm."

I couldn't take my eyes off the dragon. He began to shift back again. It was hard to see exactly how it happened in the waning light, but within a few seconds, a naked Maddox stood where the dragon just was, holding his hands over his privates. My body trembled, rejecting the notion of what I'd just seen.

Ava shaded her eyes and tossed his jeans off the deck railing to him. Maddox caught them and tugged them on, then lurched toward me with concern on his face. "Artemis didn't mean to do that. He was trying to help."

I slid sideways toward the door but didn't realize Maverick was in the way. Suddenly, I felt like a bunny cornered by predators. "Stop," I said forcefully, the way we were taught as teenagers when approached by someone we feared wanted to rape or kill us. "Don't come any closer."

Tiptoeing around Maverick, I darted in the door. "Stay out there," I yelled. "I need to breathe and take care of Tiffany's arm."

Hailey stood in the kitchen with a crestfallen look on her face. She reached for Tiffany, but I hugged her tighter. "No," I said. I tried to inch past her without touching her.

They were all tainted now like they had a disease. They'd known all this time, all of them.

And if it was all Kingstons, that meant Jury was a freak like them, too. And that meant Abby knew.

She'd become one of my best friends. How was it possible that she hadn't told me? A real friend would have warned me. Broken it to me gently that the man I was sleeping with was a ravenous murdering beast.

I locked Tiffany in the bathroom with me and turned on the water. "Wash your arm, baby." As I pumped antibacterial soap all over her arm, the tears began to fall.

"Mommy, don't cry." Tiffany patted my arm with her wet, soapy hand. Ignoring her, I scrubbed her scratched arm with my hands and tried to combat the panic rising in my throat. As I rinsed her arm, my emotions went into full meltdown mode. Because why not? If shifters were real, I had the right to melt down. If shifters were real, then this should've been my fairy tale.

Cinderella, I was not. I bit back my sobs and gave myself a few minutes to fully cry and freak then mopped up my face. I used Ava's hand towels to neaten up my makeup and cool off my hot face after crying.

Tiffany tried to comfort me the whole time. Eventually, I got her arms dried and blotted her clothes where the water had splashed. I straightened my clothes and prepared to walk out with Tiffany in my arms. I wanted to get to my car and get home as soon as I could. These creatures were clearly a danger. I couldn't have that around my baby.

"Mommy?" Tiffany looked at me with big, pleading eyes. "Can I have a pet dinosaur?"

I burst out laughing but choked it back as fast as I could. It was time to try to leave, and that meant facing them. Nothing about this was funny.

But when we stepped out, everyone looked at us. The bathroom was directly across from the open living room. They all sat on the couch, with Hailey in the armchair. That left the loveseat for Tiff and me.

Maddox had fully dressed, but he looked like he was about to come out of his skin. Ha. That was ironic. Just seeing him terrified me all over again. Now that I knew what he was, what he was capable of, how could I ever look at him the same again? He'd already hurt Tiffany. Yeah, it was probably an accident, but there was way too much unexpected with a creature that had claws and could breathe fire.

I assumed they could breathe fire. Part of me was curious, but no way I was about to ask. I wasn't even sure I was going to sit down and let them try to explain further. This was too damn much. My child had been through too much in her short life already, losing her father the way she had. I couldn't subject her to this insanity, too.

"Are you okay?"

Might as well be honest. "No. No, I'm not. I can't be here. I can't have Tiffany here. It's not fair to subject her to this."

"To what?" Maddox asked. "I wanted to keep it from her, at least until she was older. Until she could understand."

"This is no way to raise a child," I said. "I can't face this."

"That's not fair," Maddox said. "I'm still the same person. I haven't changed. I just revealed more of myself to you. And like I said before, I'd never, ever intentionally hurt you or Tiffany."

"I get that. I do. But this is too much to process." I looked at Ava. "A family of dragon shifters would be shocking to anyone."

Ava shrugged. "I fainted. But Beth, I promise you, Maddox is still the man you fell in love with. He's not someone else because he has a part of himself that you didn't know about." She smiled at Maverick. "They have control of the animalistic sides of themselves. They aren't raging beasts. They're sentient and intelligent. Hell, sometimes I think their dragons are more intelligent than the guys are."

Maverick rolled his eyes but nodded. "She's probably right."

"I can't accept it." I still hadn't left the bathroom doorway or gone any closer.

"Artemis is a part of me. I can't give it up. It's not like I'm a prince who can abdicate the throne. He's a package deal with me like Tiff is with you."

"That's a huge false equivalence," I said. "Not the same at all. Tiffany is a baby. Artemis is a damn beast. I can't trust a dragon!"

"Then you can't trust me." Maddox's eyes filled with tears.

But I nodded. "After this? You springing this on me? No. It's true. I can't trust you."

Ava leaned forward as if to say something, but Maverick put a hand on her back.

Enough was enough. "This is too much, Maddox, I'm sorry, but I'm not up for something like this. We have to break it off."

He looked like he was ready to vomit, but he didn't fight me. "I'll do whatever is best for you. I love you, and whether you believe it or not, so does Artemis. He chose you." The tears in his eyes fell, but I'd cried myself out in the bathroom. "You're breaking our hearts," Maddox whispered. "Artemis didn't think you'd reject us."

It majorly creeped me out, the way he talked about them as if they were two separate beings. It was too much. His words didn't sit right with me.

"I understand if you need to go." His voice sounded so broken it made me wonder if I was overreacting, but my fear couldn't be ignored. I nodded and turned toward the door. At the last second, I looked back.

Maddox stared down at me. "I love you, even if you can't love all of me." He walked forward, but I didn't run this time. I didn't think he'd hurt me, not in his human skin. He kissed the top of Tiff's head before he turned and walked down the hall toward the kitchen. A few seconds later I heard the back door slam shut.

"I'm sorry," I whispered to Ava and Maverick. Hailey had big crocodile tears rolling down her cheeks.

As fast as I could, I ran out the door and down the steps. My hands shook with adrenaline and fear as I strapped

Tiffany in. Being out in the dark, knowing dragons were out there and could've been stalking me made my heart pound, and fear danced along my spine.

My window was cracked, and the night air streamed in as I drove a bit too fast down the driveway. In the distance, a roar reached my ears. It was faint, but I could've sworn it sounded like pain. Not anger. Like he was heartbroken.

My hands shook as I turned toward home. Heartbroken dragon or not, I had to get the hell out of there.

Chapter 20 - Maddox

The week passed like a turtle on downers. I'd been trying to keep myself busy, so I didn't have to keep thinking about Beth, but it had been hard. Every time I turned around, I thought I spotted her or Tiffany. To distract myself, I picked up a few extra shifts at the station. That didn't help much at all, since that meant I was out and about more, imagining that I was catching glimpses of her. After work, still miserable, I headed up and mowed my mom and dad's lawn and then my grandparents'. I offered to do Axel's, but he said he'd just done it. It was hard to find enough to keep me distracted.

Bethany had rejected me. She feared me. She saw me as a beast, an animal. She couldn't love me for me and that hurt. More than I expected it to. It just solidified that this would never have happened if I wasn't a Kingston. I knew my family wasn't to blame, but if they weren't shifters then I wouldn't have been one either. I hated to think that way, but how could I not? I hadn't chosen this life. I hadn't been raised in it. It was thrown on me when I was nearly eighteen.

In some ways, it was amazing. I was a part of something special. A step above the rest. And most of the time I was happy to be in this life, to have a dragon. To be in this family.

This week, all I could see was the downside. All the negatives. The danger. The lack of privacy. It all piled up on me. All I wanted was a normal life. The dragon thing could be cool at times, but right now it caused me to miss the woman and child I'd fallen in love with.

Artemis was quiet and he'd been that way since Saturday. Five days now. He was devastated, not that I blamed him. Bethany had ripped out our hearts and stomped on them. Artemis chose the wrong mate, and there was no such thing as choosing someone else, as far as we all know. I asked everyone in the family, even Rico and Stefan. They all said no, that once a fated mate was chosen, that was it. Neither of us would ever be comfortable with another mate again.

My family has been walking on eggshells around me, and it just made me feel even more exposed. No matter where I went, whether it was to work or just doing yard work, someone tried to make me feel better. Everyone knew my business; everyone knew my life. I was trapped. Like being watched under a microscope.

It was all too much, and it was clear I needed to take Artemis away. Being so close to Beth but so far away was making both me and Artemis depressed. She wouldn't take my calls and when she saw me in town, she looked the other way. Then, she turned around and walked right out of the supermarket and to her car. It was clear she'd made up her mind.

And I had made up mine.

I sent out a group text to my family and asked everyone to meet me at the manor for dinner. Even Stefan. My grandmother replied and said she'd make shredded barbecue pork. Everyone else started replying with side dishes they'd bring. As if it was just another dinner with the family.

It wasn't.

I was off work and everyone's yards were mowed. I'd gone for a run, then let Artemis do some flying. And still, it was barely past lunch. I headed on up to the manor and got my truck, then drove it until I had to fill up with gas, then drove more. Finally, it was time to head back. I pulled in to find a bunch of cars and trucks already there. Good.

As I slammed the truck door shut, my grandfather walked out onto the front porch. I trudged up the stairs and met his eyes. They crinkled as he gave me a sympathetic smile. "Is this what I think it's about?"

I nodded.

"You made up your mind?" He put his hand on my shoulder.

"I did."

"Then I support you. But, son, I sure hope you're making this decision based on logic and not emotion."

I thought about what he said. I know there were a lot of emotions that went into my decision, but in the end, I didn't see how I could stay here in Black Claw when my mate was here—here without me. "I think this is best for me and Artemis."

Artemis made a pitiful sound in my mind. He was beyond sad. I had to do something to lift his spirits.

We walked into the living room where Hailey had the babies, playing with them. My grandmother kept lots of toys here at the manor and had them all pulled out for the kids. All the parents always slipped Hailey some money when she babysat the various babies that were in the family now, so she especially loved doing it. Though, if I knew my sister, she would've done it for free.

We continued into the kitchen where the chatter I'd heard while walking through the house died off instantly. My entire family looked at me with anxiety and sympathy.

"Come on in." My mom jumped up from the table. "Come on, honey, I'll load you up a plate."

It normally bugged me when she tried to baby me like that, but I just sat down and let her do it today. In a few minutes, I had a plate loaded down with a barbecue sandwich and lots of side dishes.

I dug in, ignoring everyone's curious glances. I knew they were dying to find out why I'd asked them here, but I wasn't ready to answer them. Instead, I ate.

When I was so stuffed that I couldn't cram one more bite in, I set down my fork and sighed. Nobody else was still eating. And it was an understatement to say they looked about ready to jump out of their skin.

I felt like I was going to vomit up all the food I'd just eaten, but I sucked in a deep breath and got it over with. "You all know I've been accepted to law school."

"No," Mom whispered. "Don't tell me you've decided not to go."

I chuckled and shook my head. "I'm still going. But I was accepted to a prestigious school in California. And I think I'm going to accept it. No, I know I am." I sucked in a deep breath while they stared at me in stunned silence. "I've decided to go to law school in California," I said firmly.

Nobody said anything. I glanced at my mom to find tears in her eyes. "How long have you known?"

This was the question I had hoped she wouldn't ask. I sighed and met her eyes. "A few weeks." More like several weeks, but no need to clarify, really.

"Why didn't you tell us? We don't keep secrets in this family." She looked more upset than I'd seen her since we left her ex-husband.

Her pain hit me in the heart and guilt washed over me. "It's hard to keep anything to myself these days," I muttered, feeling defensive. "I didn't know what I was going to do. I didn't want to say anything until I was sure."

She glared at me, and the rest of the family watched me with a mixture of sympathy and sorrow.

"Lately, I feel like I have no privacy. It can be overwhelming sometimes when I really just want to work on things on my own. I love you." I looked around the huge dining table. "I love you all. But I have to do this."

My announcement hurt their feelings. That much was obvious. "I'm sorry," I whispered.

"Don't be sorry, son." My dad, sitting beside me, put his hand on my shoulder. "I didn't think about how much your life was going to change after finding out you were a shifter. You had no time to prepare for it. You found out just a few short months before your first shift. We all had our entire lives to get there."

He gripped the back of my neck as my eyes prickled with tears. I was so relieved that he understood.

"Do what you need to do to have peace of mind. You have all my support. We'll make it work."

He stood and pulled me up, then wrapped his arms around me. My throat choked up and only got worse when I felt and sensed more hands on me. We were in a giant group hug, and it wasn't hokey or corny. It was loving. Supportive. It made me wonder if I'd made the wrong choice.

"It's okay, Maddox. We're here for you," Axel said. "Whatever you need."

Someone squeezed my shoulder. "I'll help you move. And Abby and I would love to visit California," Jury said.

"You'll be okay," Mom said. She wiggled her way to my front and hugged me tightly. "Whatever it takes for you and Artemis and your heart to heal. We want you to be whole."

She squeezed me tighter. "I'm always Team Madd. I've known since you were a little boy that you are destined for great things, Maddox. I'm so proud of you for getting into a second law school."

I couldn't help it. I clung to her and let the tears fall. Having my mom's arms around me made me feel like a little boy again like she could solve any problems in my life just by being my mom.

I knew damn well I was lucky to have my family. They'd always be my family and have my back, no matter where in the world I was.

It was time for me to go.

Chapter 21 - Bethany

My eyes kept unfocusing and the black words blended into the white background on the page. It had been like this for a week and a half. Every day harder than the last.

The first few days after finding out Maddox's huge secret, I was furious. He'd betrayed me by making me fall in love with him without telling me this massive bit of information about himself.

But by Wednesday or Thursday of last week, I was beginning to waffle. By the time Saturday rolled around and it had been a full week, I'd moved from angry and hurt to questioning to full-blown curious.

Now, Tuesday found me in overwhelming regret and guilt. Maddox had this massive secret, and if all the romance novels ever written were any indication, he couldn't tell just anyone. If anyone and everyone knew, the whole world would know, and it would've been common knowledge.

It definitely was not.

Therefore, it stood to reason that they saved telling the secret for the most intimate people in their lives. I'd become one of the people most intimate with Maddox, and he'd decided he wanted to share this massive secret with me, and I'd ruined it by stomping all over his heart. And his dragon's.

His dragon's.

Artemis.

His name was burned into my memory. Tiffany had picked up on it somehow during the chaos that happened that night and she'd been repeating it all week. She said he was her new pet dinosaur and kept asking when we could go pick him up. That really didn't help.

With a sigh, I tried to read the page again. And once again, the words blended together. "Snap out of it!" I yelled at myself. Hopping up, I pushed my desk chair back and jumped up and down a few times. Then, I shook my whole body and rolled my neck, trying to get my blood pumping.

I'd been on so many walks and hikes this week I'd lost count. Getting blood pumping wasn't doing the trick. Apparently, only time would fix my problem of the overwhelming guilt making me unfocused.

After moving around for a few minutes, I sat back down and tried to read the contract again. I'd been looking for a new contract template online since I had trouble with the last tenant.

Thirty minutes later, I grunted in frustration and gave up. Focusing was way too damn hard. I wasn't sure how many times I'd read the same paragraph about holes in walls. At least I'd been able to pick up on what the paragraph was about.

As normal, I neatened up my desk and left my office in perfect order before walking out the back door to my car. I figured I'd go pick up Tiffany and take her to the park. Or maybe hike with her, she was old enough to get to the first waterfall without fatigue. I'd tried taking her about a year ago, but I'd ended up having to carry her most of the way back.

As I pushed the button to unlock the car, my phone rang in my pocket. I checked the caller ID. "Hey, Mom," I said in a fake cheery voice. "What's up?"

The sound of police sirens in the distance grew louder, making it difficult to hear my mom, but I picked up that she was very upset. "Mom? I can barely hear you!"

The sirens got incredibly loud. They must've been on my street or one street over. They stopped suddenly and Mom's voice yelled through the phone. "Tiffany has been kidnapped!" she screamed.

My world shifted. The ground shook under me, and as Mom's words registered, Maddox ran around the corner of the house in his uniform. "Tiffany," I whispered.

All the blood in my body rushed to my head. I was sure I was going to hit the ground. But then, Maddox's arms were around me, holding me up. The world stopped shaking and my mother's voice came into focus again.

"Mom?" I didn't push Maddox away. I was able to focus on my mother's voice, but only Maddox's arms were keeping me upright. "What happened?"

Maddox guided me to a bench near the house. I'd been meaning to pressure wash it and spray paint it to make a seating area back here but hadn't gotten around to it.

"We were at the park. Walter Bearth appeared out of nowhere. He had a gun! He looked drunk and screamed at me that he has rights to his granddaughter and how we weren't going to keep her from them."

It was a good thing I was already sitting down because I would've lost my footing hearing about the gun. "He took her?"

"Yes! He threatened to shoot me if I tried to stop him, then he had his gun on Tiffany when I still tried to stop him anyway. He said he'd kill her before letting her come back with us." She sobbed while Maddox held me close. His chest rumbled with a near-constant growl. I knew it was Artemis reacting to Tiffany being taken.

"I need you to trust me." Maddox pulled back a little. "I'm going to get our girl back."

My chest pounded and ached. It became harder and harder to suck in a full breath. Maddox put his hand on the back of my neck and shoved me down until my head was stuck between my knees. Sobs wracked through my body. If I'd been with her, I could've prevented this. If I'd answered the calls from Kyle's parents, even just one of them, Walter wouldn't have felt the need to go to such extreme measures.

Oh, God, Tiffany had to have been terrified. She didn't know Walter or Mary. I never, ever brought her around people without me unless she knew them and was comfortable with them. I wouldn't have even considered leaving her with Ava yet.

"This isn't your fault." Maddox rubbed my back. "Breathe."

How did he know I was feeling extreme guilt?

"Bethany," Maddox said in a serious voice. "They've been spiraling. This isn't on you."

I nodded and sat up. He was right. The blame rested solely on Walter and Mary's shoulders. The fear settled in my gut, but I had to focus and keep it together. I couldn't help Maddox find Tiffany if I was completely in meltdown mode.

"You went the legal route. You did all you could." He continued to rub my back, but it occurred to me that while we sat here with me losing my damn mind, Tiffany was with drunk Walter.

"He could've already driven off the road," I whispered.

"What?" Maddox looked at me in concern.

"Mom said Walter appeared drunk." I jumped up and ran to the side of the house. It must've been Maddox's sirens I heard.

He scrambled to follow. "What are you doing?" he called. Within seconds, he'd caught up to me at the passenger side of the police cruiser.

I yanked on the handle, but the door was locked. "Let's go!" I exclaimed. Images of Tiffany thrown from a car because she wasn't in a seatbelt ran through my mind. I saw her being dragged away, kicking and screaming, as Walter waved a gun. "Come on, Maddox, now."

"Okay, I got it." He pulled the keys out of his pocket and stuck the key in the lock. "Get in. I was going to get Abby to come over and sit with you while I went to the station to figure out the next moves. I know what I'd like to do, as a member of the Kingston clan, but we have to go the legal route."

I slid into the car and sucked in deep breaths while Maddox walked around. The fear coursing through me threatened to overwhelm me again, but I slammed my fists down on my knees a couple of times.

"Hey, whoa," Maddox said. He put his hand on my left fist. "Talk to me."

He backed quickly out of my driveway and headed down the road.

"I don't know what to talk about," I whispered.

"Tell me about Tiffany," Maddox said. He turned on the sirens. They were louder than I expected.

"Uh, she's smarter than I expected a child her age to be," I called. "I keep checking online and looking for milestones and what a normal three-year-old should be able to do."

Maddox turned onto Main Street and nodded. "She's advanced?"

"I think so. I was going to bring it up to her pediatrician at her four-year physical."

We didn't encounter any other vehicles until we got onto Main, and luckily it darted into a parking lot, so we were able to hurry down and pull in behind it.

Maddox rushed around the car to meet me at the front and took my hand. "Come on."

"Why are we here?" I asked as we ran into the station. "Shouldn't we be searching for Walter?"

"We've got deputies doing just that," Maddox said. "Don't worry."

As soon as we walked into the station, I stopped short after hearing a shrill cry. My mom slammed into me. Maddox had to brace me again as I staggered backward from the force of my mother's embrace.

"Bethany, I'm so sorry! I should've protected her. How could I have let her get across the playground from me, knowing Walter was after her?"

Part of me wanted to yell at her that she should've been closer. She could've protected Tiffany. But I knew that was unfair. I didn't stand right on top of Tiffany when she played. Not even after she almost fell off the monkey bars. "Mom, it wasn't your fault. You know I don't like helicopter parenting. I wouldn't have been right on top of her myself if I'd been the one there."

Maverick pulled Maddox aside and they conferred very quietly. I continued consoling my mother. At first, I considered that she should've been the one comforting me, but seeing her granddaughter kidnapped had to have been traumatizing for her.

After a few moments, Maddox walked away from his father and touched my arm. "Can I speak to you for a second?"

I nodded and Maverick put his hand on Mom's arm. "Let me get you a cup of coffee."

She nodded absently. "Sure, yeah."

There was nobody else at the station. I assumed they were all out searching for Tiffany. "What is it? Do you have a lead?"

"I know you're very uncomfortable with what you found out about me," he said. "But it can help us."

"What, can you track while shifted?" I asked.

He nodded. "Yes."

My jaw dropped. "No shit?"

"No shit. And better than that, Jury is a sort of specialized tracker. He has a gift. He's already out looking, but he hasn't shifted. But for us to do this, we have to be discreet.

In our town especially, we can't have anyone discovering our secret."

I nodded. "What do you want me to do?"

"Call your father. He's with Carlos, one of our deputies. He insisted on riding along. Convince him your mother needs him. He's the main reason we haven't shifted already."

I yanked my phone from my pocket. "Of course."

Dialing Daddy's number, I shifted from foot to foot as it rang. He picked up just as I was about to give up and call again. "Pumpkin? Is there news?"

"No, Daddy, but Mom's nearly hysterical. You've gotta let them bring you here to calm her down. Let the police do their job and find Tiffany. We don't have any business out there with them."

"I can help, Bethany."

"Daddy." I didn't leave any room for argument. "Come to the station. Now."

He paused, then sighed. "Okay. I'll come."

I nodded at Maddox, who gave his father a significant look.

"Okay, Daddy, hurry. Mom needs you."

He relayed the info to Carlos, who took the phone. "Tell Maverick I'm bringing Mr. Leeds to the station right now, and there will be no civilians on the case." He gave me coordinates, which I rattled off to Maddox. He nodded.

After I hung up, Maddox pulled me into his arms. "Trust me," he whispered. "We'll find her."

"I don't care how. Get my baby back." I trusted that he would. It was funny, I'd been so terrified of them before. Now I trusted he could do exactly what I needed him to do.

As he and Maverick ran from the station, I knew it was to turn into flying dragons and find my daughter. And I knew she'd be beyond delighted to see her pet dinosaur.

It would be okay. It had to be.

Chapter 22 - Maddox

When Bethany's mom had come running from the park, bursting into the station with other witnesses, I'd been ready to rage. But I kept my head while Dad got all the witness statements. I'd wanted to shift immediately and track down the fucker who'd taken my little girl.

But we had to follow human laws. This was a human problem. For all anyone could ever know, we had to find her the proper way. Of course, we'd be using our preternatural senses to track him down, but all the reports, everything on paper had to say we lucked out and got a lead. We'd figure out later what that lead was.

Jury was driving around. I'd called him on the way to pick up Bethany. He couldn't shift and search that way, but his nose was still a step above the rest even when human. He was trying to pick up Walter's trail even in his vehicle.

As soon as I walked outside, my Dad looked at me. "Be smart. Be stealthy. You cannot be caught, so you absolutely must keep a level head."

I gave him a somber look. "I will. I know the importance."

He squeezed my shoulder, then took off toward the park to coordinate with Grandpa, Uncle Axel, and Carlos and his wolves. They were all on foot, searching for information or scents. "Hey, meet me at the manor. We can shift and stay in the woods. Try to pick up the trail."

"You got it. I just started over at the park. I keep losing the scent because of Walter's car. It's got an oil leak and the smell is overpowering. If I can shift, I can discern the scents."

"I'm at the station," I said. "Pick me up."

He was close. He pulled into the station parking lot about two minutes later and I hopped into his truck. "Did Bethany give the okay?" he asked. "To call off her old man?"

I nodded. "Yeah, they're on their way back to the station so we can get out there into the woods and shift."

He drove fast down Main Street. He wasn't in a cruiser, so we had to wait for a couple of cars to get out of the way, but as soon as we hit the woods on the family driveway, he pulled over. We ran into the woods on the park side of the driveway and stripped. stuffing our clothes into my neck bag. "Take the lead," I said. "Focus on Tiffany. I'll focus on keeping us hidden."

Jury nodded and we both shifted quickly. Artemis and Nyx roared quietly at each other before Nyx took off through the trees. We moved with a combination of running, jumping, and propelling ourselves forward with our wings. We were far too bulky to be able to properly fly inside the tree line. Having to hide like this slowed us down, but it was still faster than trying to do it as humans.

Even though I was supposed to be watching for any stray humans in our forest this close to the main roads, I caught a whiff of Tiffany. I nudged Artemis, who spoke to Jury through his dragon. Jury had the scent in seconds and took off. We had to stay in the woods, but we followed the road until it branched off onto a side parking lot.

I was beyond thankful the trail didn't lead back toward town or into the next county, where I was pretty sure Kyle's parents lived. We were still in Black Claw, and technically still on Kingston land, though it stopped at the road.

We had to cross the street. I stuck my head out and checked up and down the street. When I was sure it was clear, we launched ourselves across the road and into the woods there. We were officially off of Kingston land and toward the area I used to like to hike before Bethany almost caught me.

When the scent was so strong that I was afraid I'd run right into them shifted, I stopped and changed back, quickly pulling clothes out of the bag. Jury shifted too and dressed. "We're very close."

A woman's shrill voice caused both of us to step forward as quietly as we could.

"Damn you, Walter!" Mary Bearth cried.

I spotted Tiffany's grandfather on the other side of a SUV and pulled my phone out of my bag. First, I made sure it was on silent, then texted my father exactly where we were. He'd know the place, but he'd be lucky if he got here before I killed the old man.

Tiffany was in the driver's seat, clearly crying. Artemis and I reacted viscerally. I let out a growl I didn't even mean to. Walter whirled around to look into the woods.

"Walter!" Mary yelled. She must not have heard me growl like he did. "This is not what Kyle would've wanted. I can't believe you did this. You told me you were just going to try to talk to Bethany's mother, get her on our side. You never said anything about grabbing Tiffany! You've made me a kidnapper."

"Kyle can't say what he wants, can he? He can't decide how his daughter should be raised. He's gone!" Walter still had the gun in his waistband. "You give me back the keys. Now!"

So Mary had gotten the keys from him. That was good. Otherwise, there was no telling how far away they could've gotten by now.

Tiffany sobbed harder, and I wanted nothing more than to take Walter's head off. Slowly.

Sirens in the distance made Walter and Mary panic. They were about to jump back in the car. Mary threw Walter the keys. "We have to take her back!" she screamed.

"I won't!"

Mary grabbed Tiffany out of the front seat. I growled again, dangerously close to shifting as Artemis took control of our throat and let out a true dragon roar. They both froze, then Mary practically threw Tiffany into the back seat. Walter tripped over his own feet in his haste to get in the driver's seat. They obviously had no idea what sort of predator was in the woods, but they wanted no part of it. Not to mention the sirens. Unfortunately, I couldn't let them leave.

As I was about to dart out of the woods and try to arrest them without my gun, I heard a car on the gravel lane that led to the highway. Then my father's cruiser came into view, blocking off the road. But he had to be careful. He knew Walter was armed.

Sure enough, when Walter realized he couldn't go out to the main road, he jumped out of the SUV with his gun pointed toward the cruiser.

Looking at Jury, I nodded my head into the woods. "We can go around and surprise him from behind."

He tapped his nose in acknowledgment and we tiptoed through the woods, keeping our eyes on Walter. At some point, we passed the point that he could see us as my father tried to negotiate with him. In the meantime, more police cars pulled up with my grandfather and Uncle Axel, plus Carlos. When we were sure we wouldn't be detected by Walter, we exited the woods and ran on light feet toward his back. I pointed to the left. Jury nodded and pointed to the right. We split, each of us taking one of Walter's arms. Mine was the left, the one that held his gun. Without giving him any warning, I sprang on him and thrust his arm upward, using my superior strength to take the gun out of his hand.

Jury took his right hand around and behind his back. "I got him," he exclaimed.

I unloaded the revolver and flung the bullets as hard as I could, then pressed the switch to remove the barrel from the gun as if for cleaning. Now if Walter got his hands on it again, he couldn't have used it even if he did have more bullets on him somewhere.

Mary walked around the car holding Tiffany. "I didn't want him to," she sobbed.

When Tiffany spotted me, she squealed. I rushed toward her with my heart beating out of my chest. "It's okay," I whispered. Mary gave her up without a fight.

Tiffany stopped crying the moment I had her in my arms. "Maddoth," she whispered. "Did you bring my dinosaur?"

I chuckled and buried my face in her neck. Artemis and I inhaled her scent, both of us beyond relieved she was safe.

"Okay, it's safe!" Dad yelled once he had Walter cuffed.

Mary agreed to handcuffs as well, but Axel put hers in front of her. I watched Bethany and her mother and father spring from one of the police cars toward the back of the line.

Bethany sprinted forward. "Tiffany!"

I set Tiff down and let her run to her mother, following slowly. When I reached them, I let Bethany question Tiffany over and over, but the sweet girl was unharmed. She'd been scared of the strangers, and if they'd wrecked, this would've been a far different outcome. But thank goodness, they hadn't.

"Thank you," Bethany sobbed. "Thank you so much." She reached one arm around and yanked me toward them.

I pulled both my girls into my arms. Artemis purred with happiness to have them both with us again. She stared up at him and I remembered the night at my parents' house. She may have been grateful, but she didn't trust me or accept me. Artemis didn't fight me, either. We remembered her reaction to us vividly.

I kissed Tiff's head. "Be a good girl for your mommy." Artemis was hurting and he needed to shift again. We waited until everyone was in their cars before slinking back into the woods to shift. I had to clear my mind and allow the pain I'd been keeping at bay to be released.

Chapter 23 - Bethany

Being alone made me panicky. I couldn't stand to be away from Tiffany, not for a minute. My mom figured I had some sort of post-traumatic stress. After the first night trying to stay in my house alone, I called my mom and asked her if we could come to stay with her.

Of course, she'd said yes. They'd changed my bedroom into a guest room long ago, but it was nice. My mother had long ago given Tiffany her own room at their house. The little stinker was thrilled with us staying with my parents. She thought it was like a sleepover or camping.

After the drama of the kidnapping, I'd been holding Tiff closer and spending more time with my parents. They seemed to have been more than happy having us around, so I didn't see any real reason to go home. I still went there when I absolutely had to, but only to the office. And if I knew I'd have to be alone at my house, I made sure Mom planned to stay with Dad and Tiffany, and I called Kara or Abby to meet me at the office.

Walter was in jail. They'd let Mary out after Jury and Maddox told the judge she hadn't been a willing participant, but she never went and bailed him out. Even knowing he was behind bars, I was terrified all the time. Someone else could've decided they wanted to hurt us, and how could I stop them? I was powerless, as was proven quickly by Walter.

Saturday, nearly two weeks after the kidnapping, my mother opened the guest room door. "Morning, sweetie."

I stretched and smiled at her. "Morning. Did you make breakfast?" She'd been spoiling us by making breakfast every morning. When I eventually went back home, I sure would miss it.

"Yes, but I wanted to talk to you first."

I sat up in the bed as she climbed up beside me and crossed her legs. "What is it, Mom?" She seemed concerned, but not overly worried.

"I want you to call up your girlfriends or that Maddox and go out tonight," she said.

Recoiling against the headboard, I gave her a confused look. "Why?"

"As much as your father and I love having you and Tiff here all the time, it's gone on too long. It's not good for you to stay here this long. You're hiding."

I huffed. "Mom, come on. I'm not hiding. I've been having anxiety."

"Well, you've got to face it. So, your father and I decided we're keeping Tiffany tonight and you're going out."

Her words sent a wave of worry down my spine. "I'm not comfortable being away from Tiffany."

The thump of her hand on the mattress as she slapped it made me jump. "Do you think it's my fault that Tiffany was kidnapped?"

I shook my head. "No, I don't. It could've just as easily happened to me."

"Then leave her here. We won't go out, not even to the back yard. And if anyone knocks on the door, we'll call the police."

I chuckled at her overreaction. "Thanks, Mom."

"You can't live in fear. But I also don't want you to go back to the person you were before you met Maddox. You came out of your shell with him. It was like you bloomed."

I tugged at a stray thread on the bedspread. Thinking about Maddox made me feel like a total tool. I should have shown more gratitude towards him, but I was embarrassed by the way I'd treated him, only for him to be the one to save my daughter with his "abilities". I wanted to apologize to him, but somehow the words never would come. I'd never screwed up so bad I couldn't find a way to say I was sorry. Not until I messed up with Maddox.

"Okay," I said. "I'll go out. You're right. I have to live my life."

Mom patted my hand. "And you're not doing it here." She walked out of the room. "Come eat."

I sent a text to Abby first. **I need a drink. Go out with me tonight?**

After a shower, I checked my phone to find a reply from my friend. **Hell, yes! I've got all the girls ready. See you at about eight.**

I smiled at her. Of course she did. It would probably be every girl I'd ever met in my life.

A couple of hours before I was due to meet her, I kissed Tiffany and hugged her extra tight, then put her in my Dad's lap. "Not one toe outside, okay?"

Dad saluted. "We're going to hang out in here and watch a movie, don't you worry."

I had to kiss her three or four more times, but I finally made it out and headed to my house to get ready. Since it was girls' night and not a date, I didn't spend too much time. After running a brush through my hair and a quick mascara and lip gloss application, I was good to go.

Abby picked me up. She'd texted a little bit ago and promised to be the designated driver.

I squealed when I saw the car full of people. She'd driven her SUV, and Harley was in the back seat with Kara. They'd left the front passenger seat open for me. I hopped in and grinned at my friends. "Hey!"

"Let's do this!" Harley said. "I'm ready."

Abby reached over before putting the car into gear and hugged me. "I was so glad to hear from you."

She'd tried texting me a few times after the kidnapping. "I'm sorry I've been standoffish. It wasn't intentional. I've just been kinda wrapped up in staying alone and protecting myself."

"That's understandable," Kara said. "Who wouldn't react that way?"

"But you're not alone, you know?" Abby put her hand over mine on my leg. "We're all here for you. And when Ava found out we were going out, she wanted to come and bring Charlotte. I told them to let us have tonight and see how you were, but you've got a support system, whether you realize it or not."

I squeezed her hand. "Thank you. I realize that now." Glancing into the backseat, I repeated my thanks. "I love you guys."

We made it into the bar and had our first drinks before anyone asked. "So," Harley said. "Have you spoken to Maddox?"

It had occurred to me during the time after I rejected Maddox that Abby and Harley were in deep, committed relationships with Kingston men. Well, Stefan wasn't a Kingston, but he might as well have been. They must've known.

But Kara wasn't, so I had to watch what I said. "No, not really. He found Tiffany, and I hugged him really hard, but then he looked into my eyes and backed away. He stood off to the side until we left. He didn't want anything to do with me. I'd hoped for a little while the kidnapping might've served as a reconnection, but it didn't."

Abby and Harley exchanged a look. "I'm going to hit the bathroom," Kara said a few minutes later. I'd only told her that Maddox had been accepted to a law school in another state and it had broken us up since there was no way I'd leave Black Claw.

Once she was out of earshot, I leaned across the table toward Harley and Abby. "How did you deal with it?"

They both laughed and exchanged a look. "I knew because our father is one," Abby said. "So, it was no shock for me."

"It was a total shock for me," Harley said after a snort. "It nearly undid us. But I loved Stefan too much to let it split us up." She looked horrified after she said it. "Not that you don't love Maddox," she exclaimed. "I didn't mean it that way."

"No, I understand. I do love Maddox." I looked around to make sure Kara wasn't on her way back. "But he sprang it on me, and it scared me. Then, after I rejected him... I don't think he wants to give me another chance."

Abby tapped her drink to mine. "Beth, the dragon is like part of their soul. Imagine having a part of your soul that can communicate with you. Yes, they have names and memories. They're separate beings. But at the same time, they're not. They truly are their dragons and their dragons are them. They're kind and loyal."

Harley nodded. "So protective. And fierce. There's nothing better. Having the opportunity to be with a dragon, to love one?" She shook her head and exchanged a glance with her sister. "It's a blessing."

Kara walked out of the bathroom but stopped to speak to someone she knew.

"I'm really sad you couldn't accept Maddox for who he is," Abby said. "Did you know he got accepted into law school in California?"

My jaw dropped. "You're joking. That's the cover story I told my parents and Kara. I had no idea that was actually true." The coincidence was uncanny. Of all the cover stories I could've pulled out of my ass, that was the one I'd gone with? The truth, somewhat.

My heart fluttered. I knew he would've been thrilled with the acceptance. But also, my stomach twisted into knots. California. Why did it have to be so far away? Someone turned an upbeat song on the jukebox, and it mocked me. I wasn't in the mood for a dance song, and every beat of the bass made my heart lurch. I was about to finalize the disaster I'd started nearly a month ago.

If I didn't fix what I broke, I could've lost him for good. Long distance was a possibility. I could've handled that. What I couldn't have handled him was going to California thinking I didn't love him. I had to fix this. I had to prove to Maddox that I loved him and his dragon.

Chapter 24 - Maddox

I looked around the back yard and smiled at my family. They'd surprised me with a big party to celebrate being accepted into two different law schools. As I watched my mom and dad, aunts and uncles, cousins, sister, and grandparents, I couldn't help but still feel an ache. There was a hole inside me that held a spot for Bethany.

And Tiffany.

Definitely and Tiffany. I missed hearing her chatter on about things that were important in the eyes of a toddler. Not to mention the feel of her skinny little arms around my neck and how she'd asked for her dinosaur.

Artemis would've given anything to stomp around the yard with her and roared like a dinosaur so she could laugh and play. Anything.

But that was over. Maybe one day we'd meet someone who could make us half as happy as we'd felt with Bethany and Tiffany. Possibly have a child of our own to roar for.

Nothing could fill that hole, though.

"We are so proud of you," Dad said. He and Mom sat across from me with Jury and Abby beside me at the picnic table. If our family grew any more, we'd have to buy even more tables for the manor's back yard.

Since the weather was fully into summer, the kids had set up a slip and slide. Of course, when it came to playing in the water, I considered myself just as much of a kid. I'd been in and out of the water all afternoon.

Finally, Jury and I had tired enough to go inside and change into dry clothes and eat lunch. When I was distracted, I did okay, but now that I was sitting quietly, all I could think about was Bethany.

The sound of a car coming up the gravel driveway made my ears prick. The wind was going in the wrong direction to get a whiff of our visitor beforehand, so Grandma walked through the house to greet whoever it was.

My face must've been animated when Bethany walked onto the back deck because Mom's and Dad's eyes both widened, and they whirled in their seats to see who I was staring at. My heart thumped, and Artemis whimpered inside me. We'd craved the sight of her, but it had been over a week since we'd caught a glimpse. She'd come in to sign some papers relating to the kidnapping, but that had been the only time.

She'd made no other attempts to reach out to us. If I'd thought it would do any good, I would've texted or called her, but I didn't want to keep beating a dead horse. She'd given me a small, grateful smile that day at the station. I'd figured that was going to be all I got.

Bethany spotted me immediately. She smiled, and I expected to feel more rejection coming off of her.

I stood and weaved through the tables toward her. When I got close, I was shocked. Her emotions were heavily clouded by shame and embarrassment.

I waited with bated breath as her hands fluttered at her side. She was nervous.

"I'm sorry," she blurted out. My heart soared with the possibility of a reconciliation. "I was wrong. I reacted so badly, and I treated you worse. You didn't deserve my reaction and neither did Artemis."

I thought he was going to force a shift right then; he was so happy she'd included him in her apology. "You...?" My words wouldn't come out right. I was still too shocked she was saying them.

"I love you," she said loudly. "I love you and I love Artemis. And I don't want to be apart from either of you anymore. I want you in my life and in Tiffany's life. You dropped everything to rescue her, and still, I didn't know what to say or how to say it, but you did it anyway, even after I hurt you. I'm absolutely terrified of the unknown and of taking risks. The last time I took a risk, I got Tiffany and lost my best friend. But nothing can change how I feel for you. How much I appreciate you being by my side, always being there for me." She sucked in a huge breath and kept talking. "I don't want to stand in the way of any of your dreams. Not here and not in California. We'll find a way to make it work if you still want to. If you're still game, I want to be a part of your end goal." She seemed to deflate a little and looked around at my family. "I couldn't let you leave without telling you," she whispered. "I had to make sure you knew."

My mind whirred with questions and scenarios where we could be torn apart again, but if I didn't take her into my arms, I was going to lose my mind. Surging forward, I gathered my mate—my love—close and pressed my lips to hers with a desperation I hadn't known was there. I'd known I was sad. I knew I had a hole in my heart. But I had been yearning for Bethany harder than I would've imagined possible.

She whimpered and clung to me. "I love you," I said into her mouth, my teeth hitting against hers. It was enough to wake me up a bit, and I remembered we had an audience of my entire family.

Claim her. Now.

"Is love enough?" I asked when I pulled back. "Can you fully accept this part of my life? The part that nobody else can ever know about?"

She nodded eagerly with her arms still around my waist. "You accepted Tiffany with no judgment. It really isn't all that different, is it? She's a part of me like Artemis is for you. I want the whole package, if you can forgive me for my behavior."

Artemis growled his approval, and he must've been projecting because all the men in the yard chuckled.

"I've missed you so much," I said and pulled her closer for another kiss.

"I missed you, too." She smiled up at me, and when I looked deeply into her eyes, I didn't know how long I could wait to claim her. I had to have her.

"Go." My father stepped up onto the deck. "I understand. We all do. Go."

He knew Artemis was urging me to claim my mate. He'd been there before. I grinned at him and avoided the eyes of all the other people, all my family. They knew exactly where we were going and why. That was a little gross, so I pretended they had no idea as I grabbed Bethany's arm and pulled her into the house.

"Where are we going?" she asked with a laugh as we crossed the kitchen.

"Your place," I said. "If you're going to be mine, I need to claim you."

We hurried across the living room and out the front door. "Want me to drive?" I asked.

She nodded. "Yes, please."

I hurried around to open her door, then ran back to jump into the driver's seat. Bethany was already buckled and leaning toward me when I slid in. "Hurry," she urged.

My mood and Artemis's need to claim her must've been contagious between us because I could read the lust in her eyes like it was an open book.

As I turned her car around, she reached over and put her hand on my crotch. "There's something I've always wanted to do, if you're up for it."

I looked at her in surprise as she reached for my belt buckle. I stretched and kept going slowly down the driveway as Bethany pulled my achingly hard dick out of my pants.

When her hot mouth closed over my head, I hissed and braked, worried I'd be too overwhelmed and run us into a tree. She moaned and that was nearly enough to do it. I spotted the driveway that led to Axel's property and turned right. Halfway up the driveway was a small alcove in the trees.

Bethany's SUV drove through the grass with no problem. As she licked up and down my shaft, I positioned the car behind a couple of trees. I couldn't guarantee total privacy, but it was extremely unlikely Axel and Charlotte would leave the party this early. We had some time.

I put the SUV in park, reaching around Bethany's body, then leaned my head back against the headrest and sucked in deep, calming breaths. I didn't want her to realize how close I was to squirting my hot cum down her throat.

When the tingling in my balls grew too persistent, I pulled at her shoulders. She sat up and looked around in surprise. "Oh, thank goodness."

I watched in amazement as she reached under her dress and tugged her slip of a G-string off. She waved it in front of my face for a second, then threw it in the floorboard before climbing over the gear shift. She clasped my dick, still glistening with her saliva, and positioned herself over me. She had to duck her head down low to keep from hitting the roof of the SUV, but she was short enough that I hoped this would work pretty well.

As Bethany sank down on my cock, I moaned. Her tight sheath felt like coming home after a long day. But a thousand times better. I reached up and massaged her breasts through her dress, then made quick work of unbuttoning it enough to expose her black lace bra. Running my fingers along the cups, I pushed them underneath her breasts. As soon as her dusty brown nipples were exposed, I claimed one with my mouth and the other with my fingers as she began to slide up and down on my dick.

Every time she went down, she clenched her hot pussy together, making me moan against her tit.

"You're amazing," she said. I leaned back and watched her face, eyes closed. She was focused on the feel of my cock stretching her and enjoying riding it.

"You're the one who is amazing," I whispered and stilled her hips on me. "I'm going to claim you when we both orgasm. I'll bite your neck, but instead of pain, your orgasm will be enhanced, and you'll be more connected with both Artemis and me."

"Do it," she whispered. "I'm going to come soon."

I buried my face in her chest again, but with my free hand, I slipped it between us and pressed my thumb to her clit, adding pressure to the feel of my cock inside her. As she moved, I moved with her, thrusting upward to connect with her deeper, faster, and harder.

Soon, her moans filled the car as her orgasm crested. When I was pretty sure it was imminent, I leaned forward and bit her neck, letting my sharp teeth break her skin and Artemis's magic claim our mate.

Our orgasms overwhelmed us, and I thrust upward as hard as I could while she writhed in my lap. I didn't let go of her neck until both of us floated down and out of the euphoria. Residual tremors rocked my dick as her inner walls quivered.

When we were both done, I let go of her neck and admired the gorgeous bite mark. There was a connection there that hadn't been there before. I smiled at Bethany as she stared at me in wonder. "Whoa," she whispered.

"I know." Chuckling, I pressed my forehead to hers. "Now you're mine. And I'm yours."

"We'll get through it," she said. "Together."

I pulled back and looked at my mate in surprise. "Get through what?" I asked.

"Your college. In California." She looked supportive and optimistic, but I felt her sadness through the bond.

"Oh, Bethany," I whispered. "I was only going to California because I couldn't stand to be so near you without having you. I'm staying right here with you and Tiffany. There isn't any place I'd rather be in the world."

She laughed and hugged me close. "But if your dream is to go to law school in California, I'll support you."

"Bethany, I was also admitted to a law school a few towns over. I'm not going anywhere. I'm staying here. I want to marry you. I want to raise Tiffany. I'm here, with you."

"You do have to go somewhere," she said.

I furrowed my brow and looked at her. "Where?"

Her eyes twinkled, then she lifted herself off of me and into the passenger seat again. "You've got to take me home and do whatever you did when I came again." She wiggled her eyebrows up and down. "That was amazing."

Artemis and I roared with laughter as I tucked myself back in my jeans and turned the car around. "Yes, ma'am."

Chapter 25 - Rico

"I'm hearing none of this. Find your purpose in Black Claw. Let that branch of our family influence you. You've got a long life of leadership ahead of you. You are *not* coming home until both Maverick and I are convinced you're ready, and that's that." My grandfather slammed the phone down. I pictured him in his study, behind his massive oak desk. He was one of the few people I knew of that still had an old-fashioned landline phone.

I sighed and looked down at my cell. I was miserable in Black Claw. I wanted to go back home. I had friends in Arizona. Family.

Sure, being in a small town had its perks. Mainly the women, but hell. I could've gotten women in Arizona just as easily, thanks to the Kingston good looks. Women weren't my focus.

My Uncle James had gotten me a job at the local auto body shop. I didn't know how to do much in life, but I could work on motorcycles. It kept me busy and away from trouble, which I seemed to be able to find no matter what was going on. Back in Arizona, it didn't seem to matter, I'd find a way to get myself into trouble.

Here, not so much, except I'd been bored out of my freaking mind. My Uncle James and Cousin Maverick were two men I had no desire to cross, so I did exactly as I was told as much as I could.

The only thing they didn't seem to mind me doing was going to the local bar for a few beers after work as long as I didn't drive myself home.

That was not a problem. With the extra stamina from Valor, my dragon, it was nothing to walk through the woods at the end of the night back to the manor where I stayed with Uncle James and Aunt Carla.

At least she was awesome. She cooked like a dream and always had a kind word.

At first, when I came to Black Claw, I'd avoided everyone, but I'd gotten bored enough to start going out again. I hadn't missed all the looks I'd gotten from the various single women of Black Claw. I could've had my pick of the litter, but women were trouble I really didn't need right then.

I'd just gotten to the bar and sat down with a couple of guys that worked at the body shop when something strange tugged at my chest. What the hell was it? I looked around, confused by the internal struggle I didn't understand.

Valor began to growl.

Mate.

Oh, no. Not this Black Claw bullshit. I turned and walked toward the bar, trying to look straight ahead and not around at all. The moment I spotted her, it would've all been over. If I laid eyes on her, it would be an enormous problem on top of my other problems. A gigantic female problem I did *not* need. When I got my beer and got back to the table without seeing her, I decided I wasn't ready to risk it. Valor was about to go nuts under my skin, and I could only keep my head down in the bar for so long. "Guys, I'm going to head home," I said with my eyes on the tabletop. "I've got a sudden headache." I slid the beer toward one of the guys who liked the same brand. "I'll talk to you tomorrow."

I walked out of the bar with my gaze glued to my feet. I didn't have any spare time for a mate.

Maybe another time. Another life.

Not today.